THE JEALOUS ONE

Celia Fremlin

Academy
Chicago
Publishers

Copyright © 1965 by Celia Fremlin.

Published in 1985 by
Academy Chicago Publishers
425 North Michigan Avenue
Chicago, Illinois 60611

Printed and bound in the U.S.A.

Library of Congress Cataloging in Publication Data

Fremlin, Celia.
    The jealous one.

    I.   Title.
PR6056.R45J4   1985   823'.914   85-3605

ISBN 0-89733-132-X

THE JEALOUS ONE

CHAPTER I

Rosamund would never have believed that so confused a dream could yet be so vivid. There had been no sense of struggle, for her savagely pushing hands had seemed to meet with no resistance, as is the way of dreams. The blind rage had seemed simply to disintegrate, to become a wild wind blowing, a whirling panorama of stars in a black sky, a throbbing of mighty sound, as of waves crashing with frightful nearness. And there, in the thunderous centre of it all, had been Lindy's hated, beautiful face, hurtling away into the darkness. Lindy's face, ugly and terrified at last!—the dream-Rosamund had registered, with terrible dream-glee; and even in the very moment of waking, the glee remained—a dreadful, pitiless exaltation. "I've won! I've won!" she began to cry aloud—but, after all, it wasn't a cry at all: just a painful rasp of sound in her sore, aching throat. The thunder of unknown seas narrowed itself down to a dull throbbing in her own head; the star-seared darkness became the chequered light from the street lamp on the walls of her bedroom, where night seemed to have already fallen while she slept.

Of course. I've got 'flu, Rosamund remembered. No wonder I'm having extraordinary dreams. Through the throbbing in her head, the roaring in her ears, she tried to sit up . . . to remember. . . . And now, as she raised herself, it was forced upon her reviving consciousness that she was not properly in bed at all, but just lying on top of the eiderdown, fully dressed. And she was cold, icily cold. She must have flopped down here exhausted after finishing the essential housework this morning—or was it early afternoon?

I wonder if I've still got a temperature? she mused dazedly and reached out towards the bedside lamp. With the sudden glare of light, full reality ought to have been switched on too; and yet her recent dream seemed to cling about her still, even as she sat up. Her whole brain, her body itself, seemed still to throb with the terrible triumph of her dream victory; she felt again that incandescent flash of evil joy as she watched Lindy hurtling to disaster—her beauty, her sweetness, her serenity, about to be eclipsed for ever.

Oh, the glory of it! Oh, the perfect, exquisite pay-off, fierce and unarguable, like the dream wind whistling and screaming through her hair!

For a moment Rosamund was almost in the dream again; but she forced her eyes open once more onto the circle of bright, real light, took the thermometer from its case, and put it into her mouth.

What had her temperature been this afternoon? She couldn't remember—couldn't, indeed, remember having taken it at all, though she must have, else how could the thermometer have been lying here, all ready, beside the bed?

How sad it was, it suddenly occurred to her, to be lying here, all alone, taking one's own temperature every four hours! As she reclined against the pillows, waiting immobilised for the appointed two minutes, Rosamund allowed herself, as a sort of invalid's treat, to be flooded by self-pity. A year ago—even six months ago—it wouldn't have been like this. A year ago Geoffrey would have been anxious about her, full of sympathy and affection. He would have noticed first thing in the morning that she was ill, and would have fussed and worried delightfully; bringing her breakfast in bed, dashing home in his lunch hour to see how she was; and by now he would have cooked her a dainty little meal, and over the bedside light he would have draped his old red scarf to protect her eyes from the glare. The last time she had been ill he had done this, and she remembered how she had lain lapped in rosy light, cradled triumphant in her illness, like a queen upon her throne.

The aching in her head grew worse as she blinked back the slow, dull tears, half stupefied by her longing for Geoffrey. Not Geoffrey as he was now—polite, and dutiful, and ill at ease—but Geoffrey as he had been once—

Geoffrey as he had been through all the long years until Lindy came to live next door.

Half past nine, and he still wasn't in! How heartless he was! As part of her solitary little treat, Rosamund was allowing herself to be unreasonable, too, as well as self-pitying. Because it was unreasonable, she knew it was, to expect Geoffrey to cancel his late night when he didn't even know she was ill.

But he *should* have known, protested the spoilt, childish bit of Rosamund's mind, and she sucked at the thermometer like a baby sucking at a dummy, for comfort without sustenance. He *shouldn't* have been so easily deceived when she pretended she was perfectly well this morning, and got up as usual and began bustling round the kitchen. He should have seen she was forcing herself to it—driving herself to the limits of her strength in order not to play the part of the malingering wife—the wife who manufactures an illness in the hopes of recapturing through pity what she can no longer claim through love.

And it's not *fair*, I really *was* ill, there was no question of malingering, thought Rosamund, weakly indignant. As if her temperature would provide the final answer to all her problems, she whipped the thermometer from her mouth and peered at it under the light, twisting and turning it this way and that to bring the magical silver thread into existence . . . the little silver messenger from another world . . . he loves me . . . he loves me not. . . .

Nearly 102°. Rosamund was pleased that her temperature was so high. It sort of accounted for—well, everything. For feeling so depressed and ill-used: for thinking that Geoffrey ought to be back already when he wasn't: and for having had that awful dream about poor Lindy. Fancy dreaming of pushing Lindy off a cliff or whatever it was—yes, it must have been a cliff because of the waves crashing and the wind howling—and then being so pleased about it—not the least bit shocked or frightened, as you would be in real life if you found you'd murdered a neighbour you disliked.

Disliked? Well, she did dislike Lindy, of course; hated her often. Who wouldn't, in her situation? But—and this was really what had made it all so peculiarly painful—her dislike had never succeeded in blinding her entirely to Lindy's many virtues. Lindy was fun; she was gay, and vital, and full of originality. She could often be kind, too, in her own way, every now and then showing a surprising degree of shrewd understanding for those in trouble. You could not even say that she had deliberately set out to hurt Rosamund, or deliberately tried to break up her marriage. And indeed she wasn't breaking it up. What was happening was something much slighter than that—much more difficult to put into words. Just a look in Geoffrey's face, really; a sort of buoyancy in his voice when he embarked on a sentence into which he was going to bring Lindy's name; a way of glancing at Lindy's house instead of at his own as he unlatched the front gate in the evenings.

But none of it was Lindy's fault, anyway. It never was the other woman's fault really, Rosamund assured herself, with fierce modernity. It was the wife's fault, always, if she so failed to please her husband that he was driven for solace to some other woman. If she was to hate anyone for the present situation, it would be more reasonable to hate herself, Rosamund reflected . . . and then, once again, the feeling of the dream washed over her, and she knew that reasonableness didn't come into it at all, never had and never could. The voice of reason was thin and tiny, like a caged canary chirping, among the savage thunders of her dream. The sense of mortal struggle was back with her again . . . the clutching, desperate hands . . . the joy of victory. How real, how vivid, fever can make a mere dream . . . !

And after all, here was Geoffrey back! Rosamund heard his feet bounding up the stairs with anxious haste. Had he, after all, suspected that she was ill this morning?

Rosamund half rose from the bed in confused hope as the door burst open, and she felt her head spinning. Surely his kind, tired face looked more worried, more dismayed, than even her wildest vanity could have warranted? He seemed hardly to see her—certainly not to notice that she had been lying down.

"Rosamund! I say!" he exclaimed tensely. "Have you any idea what's happened to Lindy? She's disappeared!"

CHAPTER II

In actual fact, of course, Lindy never had been beautiful. When Rosamund had first seen her, flushed and untidy, leaning into the back of the removal van to explain something to the men rootling about inside, she had summed her up as a rather dumpy, fussy little woman. "Woman," mark you, not "girl", was the word that had sprung to her mind at that first glimpse, when she and Geoffrey had been peeping, guiltily, like two naughty children, at the arrival of their new neighbour. It was only later that Lindy had begun to seem so young, as well as so beautiful. It was only later, too, that her house had begun to seem so beautifully and so tastefully furnished. On the day of the move, her furniture had looked absolutely dreadful, bumping its way sordidly across the pavement, every stain, every worn patch of upholstery, cruelly exposed to the blaze of a July afternoon.

"School teacher", Geoffrey had surmised cheerfully, his arm thrown lightly across Rosamund's shoulder as they both peered with companionable, ill-bred curiosity round the edge of the bedroom curtain. "School teacher, full of earnest, progressive theories about the potentialities of the young. The sort that loses her illusions late— good, sturdy, well nourished illusions, built to last. I wonder how long they'll stand up to living next door to our Peter and his pals . . . ?"

They both giggled. In those days—barely six months ago though it was—they had both been able to laugh at their sixteen-year-old son's shortcomings. It hadn't occurred to either of them, yet, to blame the other one for everything that went wrong. So they stood there at peace, intent and happy as children at the Zoo, watching a great clumsy greenish-yellow settee blundering hideously across the pavement. The men had to tip it at an angle to get it through the little iron gate of the front garden, and at another angle again to get it through the front door into the anonymous, echoing cavity of Next Door.

11

"Cat?" Rosamund put the eliptical question confidently, serene in the certainty that Geoffrey would understand not only the question but all its ramifications. For cats were good, in hers and Geoffrey's happily arbitrary scale of values. Cat-lovers were better—nicer—more amusing than dog-lovers, or budgerigar-lovers. Dog-lovers were sentimental, and budgerigar-lovers—well, it was rather awful to keep creatures in cages, wasn't it?

Geoffrey pursed his lips thoughtfully. "No cat," he opined, after several moments' reflection; and Rosamund felt his arm tighten very slightly round her shoulders—a gesture of recognition—of gratitude—for the total understanding which made such monosyllabic exchanges rich beyond the dreams of oratory.

"But all the same, I don't think she'll mind the guitar," he added, modifying a little the elaborate survey of the new neighbour's shortcomings which had just been completed in three words. "At least, she may *mind* it, but she'll pride herself on not making a fuss about that sort of thing. Just as good."

"Better," Rosamund pointed out. "People who pride themselves on not minding noise can be relied on to go on priding themselves, no matter how bad it gets. With people who actually *don't* mind, there's always the risk that there's *some* degree of noise that they *will* mind. And then you've had it. Car?"

"Ye-es. I'm afraid so. Probably."

Cars were bad, too. They were almost the same as not liking cats. Lots of their friends *did* have cars, of course, but it was a point against them. Geoffrey and Rosamund had often talked about it—how silly it was to drive everywhere when you might be enjoying the walk, or the luxury of being carried along by public transport with someone else having to worry about the traffic jams and the one-way streets. How bad it was for children, too, to be driven everywhere, they'd lose the use of their legs. Though Rosamund had to admit to herself that, in spite of his parents' foresight in not owning a car, Peter seemed to be making very little use of his so carefully-preserved legs these days: he'd spent practically the whole of last holidays lying on his bed reading James Bond—or, worse still, just lying there, thinking dark thoughts about the universe, which he would later enlarge on, despondently and somewhat patronisingly, while his mother tried to count the laundry. *Why can't I have one of those secretive teenagers who never tell their parents anything?* Rosamund would sometimes wonder ruefully as she tried to determine whether Life itself was a manifestation of futility as well as whether four shirts should really have cost 3/11½, and if so, how much could they possibly have been each?

Still, it was probably just a phase. The thought that everything was probably just a phase had sustained Rosamund through the sixteen years of Peter's upbringing just as religious principles had once sustained her grandmother. Something settled, and all-embracing, and totally unproveable, that's what you needed in dealing with children. . . .

A sharp nudge and a muffled spurt of laughter from her husband recalled Rosamund's attention to the scene below them. For a second they gripped each others' hands in an ecstasy of shared disapprobation. This wasn't just No Cat. It wasn't even a Dog, in the ordinary sense. No, it was much, much worse. It was a Pekinese. A sniffing, snuffling, arrogant, utterly pedigree Pekinese, titupping ridiculously up the path behind its mistress.

"Perfect!" whispered Geoffrey, squeezing Rosamund's hand exultantly; and, "Won't it be fun to complain of the yapping!" commented Rosamund, giggling delightedly. "Shush!" she amended, dodging back behind the curtain. "She'll hear us!"

It really was the most shocking, vulgar behaviour, spying and jeering like this. But how delightful, how utterly forgiveable, shocking behaviour did become when *both* of you were engaged on it. And anyway, there was no malice in it. Neither of them had the least thing against their new neighbour really—didn't know a thing about her yet, in spite of the guessing game which it was such fun to play.

"Let's invite her to supper tonight," suggested Rosamund impulsively. "She's sure to be in a frightful muddle, with the electricity not wired up, or something, and all the shops shut till Monday. You go and ask her, Geoffrey—right now, while she's still in and out of the front door, so that you won't have to ring the bell or anything. We don't want to make too much of a thing of it."

Geoffrey looked at his watch. He often did this when
in doubt about something, however little relevance the
time of day had to the question in hand.

"Well—I don't know," he said reluctantly. "Aren't
we busy, or something?"

Rosamund gave him a little push. "You *know* we're
not, darling!" she exclaimed. "You *know* we're only going
to do what we always do on Saturday afternoons—sit in
deckchairs, talking about you perhaps mowing the lawn."

"But I *like* sitting in deckchairs talking about me perhaps mowing the lawn," protested Geoffrey longingly;
but Rosamund continued to steer him relentlessly towards
the stairs.

"Go on. It's only neighbourly. And besides, we'll find
out all about her," she encouraged; and as soon as Geoffrey was gone, she went into the kitchen to decide what
to prepare for their unknown guest this evening.

Something cold, of course. Everybody liked cold food
best in this weather. At least, anybody who didn't know
very well that they were in the wrong. Salad, then. Salad,
and cold meat, and stewed fruit. A bit dull, perhaps, but
then Geoffrey and Rosamund had never believed in
making a great fuss about visitors. On the contrary, it
was Rosamund's custom to cook special delicacies only
when the two of them were on their own, without even
Peter. Peter, of course, was a major complication to any
meal, with his newly-acquired cynicism about food,
his enormous appetite (a most awkward combination,
for all concerned); the uncertainty about whether he
would be there at all; and, if there, whether he would have
four or five hungry (and/or cynical) friends with him.

However, he'd said he would be out this evening, for
what that was worth. She'd plan without him then, firmly,
and if he turned up unexpectedly—that is, if you could
call it unexpectedly when it happened like that two times
out of three—then he could just get something for himself.
There seemed to be a sort of limpness about teenage
arrangements today, Rosamund reflected, that she didn't
remember from her own girlhood. Surely, in her day, when
they'd planned to go out, they'd *gone* out—often in the
teeth of fierce parental opposition? Now that parental opposition was non-existent, there seemed to be left a sort
of helpless vagueness about the social arrangements of the

young, a built-in liability to cancellation or breakdown at every stage, an unerring tendency to deposit all the participants back in their parents' homes in time for some meal that one had hoped they were going to be out for.

A few years ago, when Peter was a blue-eyed, rosy-cheeked urchin who looked as if he had come straight out of a William book, Rosamund would have wanted him to be there at supper; would have wanted to show him off to this new, childless neighbour—she and Geoffrey had leapt arrogantly to the conclusion that she *was* childless as soon as they saw the Pekinese. And no doubt, one day, it would be fun to show him off again, as a handsome young man embarked on some creditable career. But for the moment it seemed better to Rosamund to boast of his existence from as great a distance as could be contrived.

The front door slammed, and Geoffrey strode through into the kitchen, smiling.

"You may down tools, dearest," he announced. "We don't have to succour the starving after all. *She's* going to succour *us*. She wants us to go in and have supper there. O.K.?"

"Well—— But——" Surprise at this turning of the tables somehow drove Rosamund into mustering objections to the plan, just as though she, and not their new neighbour, were going to have all the trouble and inconvenience of it. "But how can she? I mean, she hasn't even got the furniture in yet. . . . How can she possibly think of cooking for visitors? I mean, it must be hard enough to scratch up a meal for herself, the very first night. That was the whole idea of asking her."

"Yes, I know. I told her," said Geoffrey. "But she just laughed. She says, first things first, and it's much more important to give a party than to get the furniture straight —and honestly, Rosamund, it does look rather fun. She's been fixing candles all about on the packing cases and things, and flowers and so forth. We *will* go, won't we?"

"Well, yes, I suppose so. If you're sure she really wants us. It still seems to me an awful lot of extra work for her, just on the day of the move. . . ."

Rosamund was suddenly aware of how dull and unimaginative she was sounding, in comparison with all that lighthearted inventiveness next door. "Of *course* we'll go," she amended, smiling. "It sounds great fun. But wouldn't she like me to go in and help her, or something?"

"I don't think so. I'll ask her, if you like. I've promised to go back and run a flex for her out through the French window so that she can fix up a sort of lantern arrangement in the garden. *We* ought to do that, you know, some time. I don't know why we never thought of it. Oh, by the way, there *is* something she asked me to ask you. Have we got a piece of bright red ribbon, or something like that? She wants to make a bow for Shang Low. To celebrate their arrival."

"Shang Low?" Rosamund knew, of course, who must be the owner of this ridiculous name. Her query was a plea not for information, but for reassurance. For there should have been a note of mockery in Geoffrey's voice as he retailed this whimsical request. They had *always* jeered at Pekineses, she and Geoffrey, it was one of their things. And as for Pekineses that needed red bows for special occasions . . . !

But Geoffrey, horrifyingly, did not seem to understand. He simply answered her question.

"Shang Low—yes. The Peke," he explained easily. "Her sister had one called Shang High, you see, and really it was very appropriate, because——"

But Rosamund didn't want to hear the story. Not hear it, at least, recounted in this innocent, genuinely amused style, with no recognition of its silliness, its affectation, its typical spinsterish sentimentality. . . .

By sheer will-power, she checked the epithets piling up in her mind against the unheard and probably innocuous anecdote. Instead, she smiled.

"You'd better let her tell me the story herself," she admonished. "She will, I'm sure, and it might be difficult to laugh in the right places if I've heard it before. It's going to be quite a strain, isn't it, adjusting ourselves to Peke-type humour at such close quarters!"

She giggled in terrible solitude for a fraction of a second; and then Geoffrey joined in, a tiny bit too late and a tiny bit too loud. And the joke did not lead to another joke. Murmuring something about "having promised . . .", Geoffrey hurried away out of the kitchen and out of the house, without any red ribbon. And this piece of red ribbon, which they didn't look for, didn't find, and probably hadn't got, became the very first of the objects which couldn't ever again be mentioned between them.

CHAPTER III

Rosamund was not usually an ungracious guest. Usually she loved meeting new people, seeing their homes, learning about their lives, adding them to her rich collection of acquaintances or even friends.

But this evening, somehow, she was feeling mean. From the very moment of stepping out of the summer twilight into next-door's echoing, uncarpeted hall, she felt her whole soul bristling up, on the alert for faults and failings of any kind. So that when the door at the side of the hall opened onto a scene of sparkling prettiness, her immediate instinct was to reject it in some way—to belittle it. She found herself trying to see through and past the dancing welcome of the candle flames; beyond, above, and round the massed glory of flowers and leaves; to discern behind it all the ordinary, dull, badly-proportioned little sitting room, exactly like their own next door.

But it was impossible. The place had been turned into a magic cave, and all you could do was to forget your mean censoriousness, and surrender yourself to enchantment. Poppies, nasturtiums and great trailing sprays of leaves had made a fairyland jungle of what must really have been a hideous shambles of lumpy furniture, dumped anyhow, just as the removal men had left it. A great dusty roll of carpet loomed out of the shadows, but how cunningly those loops of ivy cast speckled lights and patterns down its length! With what a blaze of gold and scarlet did that bowl of nasturtiums surmount the scratched surface of some undistinguished table, or it might be a chest of drawers, you couldn't tell, it didn't matter. The flowers and the candles had swamped and submerged everything in one vast victory of light and colour.

"Lindy! It's superb! It's a knockout, it really is!" exclaimed Geoffrey. "Isn't it, Rosamund? Oh, but I must introduce you, mustn't I? This is my wife Rosamund,

Lindy. Rosamund, meet our new neighbour—Lindy—er . . ."
Evidently he had forgotten her surname already—or had
he never heard it? Had it been "Lindy" right from the
very first moment? Rosamund found herself shaking
hands with a sturdy-looking young woman in orange
slacks and some kind of black sleeveless garment—you
couldn't see properly in the uncertain candle-light.

"Isn't this fun!" Lindy exclaimed, seizing Rosamund's
hand with eager welcome. "I'm so glad you could come!
I was feeling so depressed, you know, and so tired, and
everything was looking so hideous and moving-day-ish,
I felt I *must* have a party! Have *you* ever felt so tired that
all you could do was give a real slap-up party, straight
away?"

Rosamund hadn't. She couldn't conceive of any other
woman ever being in such a paradoxical state of mind,
either; it was all the most outrageous affectation from
beginning to end. Impossible to say any of this, of course;
so she smiled, and said how lovely it all looked, and how
clever Lindy was to have arranged it all.

Lindy laughed, in sheer, simple pleasure at hearing
words of praise; and then suddenly her voice changed,
became low and confidential:

"Well, actually, I had another reason as well," she explained. "You see, I wanted to make things a little
cheerful for my sister, for her first evening. That's why I
was so glad you could come. She's a bit depressed, you
see, about coming here. Moving house *is* depressing, isn't
it, even at the best of times?"

"Yes. Yes, I'm sure it must be," agreed Rosamund,
trying to remember herself back into her own just-moved
state of several years ago. Had it been depressing? Or
exciting? Or just a period of minute to minute activity so
continuous as to make any sort of feelings at all seem a
ridiculous and superfluous luxury? Anyway, what was all
this about the sister?

"Your sister?" she prompted tentatively. "So she's
going to be living with you?"

"Yes. Actually, the whole thing is because of her,
really. You see, her husband's left her, poor soul, and as
I'm the free agent in the family, 1 felt it was my job to
give her a home for a bit. I mean, it seemed a bit silly,
each of us in our separate little flats, and her so lonely and

everything; so I thought perhaps this would work out better. I think it will. I hope it will."

"It sounds a good idea," said Rosamund cautiously, trying to suppress her vulgar curiosity sufficiently for good manners, and at the same time to find out lots more about the sister. "When is she coming?"

"She's here now. She's upstairs," said Lindy. "She insisted on 'getting straight', as she calls it, before she comes down. She's different from me. *I* believe in having fun first, and getting straight afterwards." She turned to Geoffrey. "Don't you agree, Geoff? If you take care of the pleasures, the pains will take care of themselves!"

She keeps a notebook of things like that, and twists them into the conversation by main force, thought Rosamund spitefully; and knew in that second that she would have to keep her spite to herself, even after the evening was over. For Geoffrey was laughing appreciatively; and so Rosamund laughed too, determined to be amused if it killed her.

And after all, it didn't kill her. On the contrary, her spirits rose, and her stimulated gaiety became genuine as she helped Lindy to slice up salami and cucumbers and hard boiled eggs, and Geoffrey plied them both with tastes of the white wine which Lindy had asked him to open —with a pair of scissors instead of a corkscrew, which of course added to the fun.

"It'll all be finished before we ever start eating," she remarked with satisfaction, peering into her empty glass. "But never mind. We'll put the empty bottle on the table surrounded by a wreath of poppies as a memento. Poor Eileen—missing it all. But she won't mind. She never drinks anyway. Where *has* she got to, I wonder?"

"Well, I suppose, if she's unpacking, it's bound to take a good while," said Rosamund, and was suddenly terrified lest the remark sounded prim. As if she was the sort of person who was on the side of people who unpacked before they started drinking white wine and scattering flowers around. "Should we help her, or something?" she added—realised that this sounded primmer still, so laughed hastily, and looked round for something gay to do, quickly; like fixing a poppy behind her ear or tossing back the last of the wine.

But as it happened she didn't need to do either, for at

that moment a kind of irritable, tentative thumping interrupted them from the direction of the door. Lindy stared for a second, then clapped her hand to her mouth in mock horror.

"There! Look what I've done! Locked out my own sister—Geoff, why didn't you *tell* me that the door wouldn't open if I put the record-player behind there?—I thought men were supposed to understand that sort of thing. *Eileen!*"—she raised her voice—"Stop battering your way in like that—you'll smash everything. Here's a kind gentleman will clear a path for you—"

Geoffrey was already on his feet and over by the door, shifting impediments, upsetting candles, and eventually creating an aperture wide enough for the entry of a neat, slim girl with high-piled hair and wide, anxious eyes.

For a moment Rosamund was taken aback. She had somehow been led to imagine an *older* sister for Lindy. The broken marriage—the "getting straight"—the non-drinking—all had combined to give an impression of downtrodden middle age. But this girl was not only younger than Lindy, she was also—at first sight, at least—a good deal prettier, with her fair complexion and masses of soft, pale hair.

"Come on, you silly girl!" cried Lindy, as her sister picked her way with perhaps unnecessary caution through the medley of deceptively-lit objects that separated them. "Come and have a drink. You must be worn out. Exhausted. You look like a ghost already. Why do you *do* it?"

Oddly, even as her sister spoke, the girl *did* begin to look rather like a ghost, Rosamund thought. You could see now that her pretty, fair skin was a little too pale, her large eyes lacking in sparkle. She seemed out of place, too—a creature out of its element, drowning, unable to breathe properly in Lindy's colourful, buoyant environment.

"Have a drink," Lindy repeated, sloshing the remains of the wine into a tumbler and handing it to her sister.

Rosamund was surprised. Hadn't Lindy just said that her sister didn't drink? Had she forgotten? Or was she just hoping to tempt her, for this once?

"No—no thanks, Lindy. You know I don't." The girl pushed the tumbler away and glanced enquiringly at the visitors. "I suppose . . . ?"

"Yes, yes, I should have introduced you, I know," said Lindy impatiently. "But it seems so silly, when you all know exactly who each other are. I've told you *all* about them, you know I have, Eileen, and I've told them all about you. Well, nearly all, anyway. Oh, well. . . . Eileen—this is Rosamund Fielding. Rosamund—this is Eileen Forbes. . . . O.K.? I needn't go through it with you, too, need I, Geoff?"

She laughed up at him in the candle-light, and he smiled down at her. "That's all right," he said. "I'll just guess. This must be—let me see—either your sister Eileen, or else your sister Eileen?"

"Wrong both times! This is my sister *Eileen*!" Lindy laughed, a high, excited sound. "But you're on the right track, you know, Geoff, there *are* several of her. Only one of them is here in this room with us. One is still upstairs, grimly sorting things, and will go on doing so all night long. Another is—ah, that's another story, isn't it, Eileen?"

She threw a merry, challenging glance sideways to her sister; but the girl did not respond. It was like throwing something to bounce off a cushion, you'd *know* it wasn't going to bounce, suddenly thought Rosamund. Just as Lindy must have known that Eileen was going to refuse the glass of wine and fail to respond to her banter. I think she's rather unkind, Rosamund's thoughts raced gleefully on, fastening with inexplicable zest onto this possible flaw in Lindy's character; she *likes* showing up her sister as much less vivacious than herself.

"Well, let's eat, anyway," cried Lindy gaily, settling herself cross-legged in front of the improvised table—an upturned drawer covered with a red-and-white checked cloth. "Who'd like Eileen's glass of wine? Who'd like to drink her health for her? Since she won't drink it herself?" She waved the glass perilously this way and that for a moment, then set it in the middle of the table. Carefully she arranged four candles round it, in a solemn square.

"There. It can be for the prize. The prize for the cleverest, the wittiest, the best at finishing the potato salad—"

She was laughing. Everyone was laughing. It was only a joke, after all. Why should Rosamund fancy she saw cruelty in the clear golden liquid thus floodlit in front of them: cruelty flickering cold and sharp among the candle flames? Was it only a figment of a censorious imagination, or had the rejected drink been set up as a laughing-stock, deliberately to highlight Eileen's lack of spirit, her wet-blanketing sobriety?

I mustn't think such things! Rosamund scolded herself, quite shocked at the headlong injustice of her imaginings, for which there was really no foundation whatever. Lindy was only acting as a good hostess—trying to make the party go. You had to say silly things when people really hardly knew each other—Rosamund should be helping her —backing her up, not sitting here criticising. Anyway, now here was Geoffrey telling one of his funny stories, telling it very well, too; even Rosamund, who had heard it a dozen times before, found herself convulsed with laughter. The meal continued happily enough, everyone spearing up food haphazard with their forks. Eileen, too, seemed to be warming a little to the situation, smiling more and more often, and allowing herself to be drawn out a little by Geoffrey's friendly questioning. She was just beginning, a little tentatively, to describe her job in the book department of a large store, when Lindy scrambled to a kneeling position, reached for the much-publicised tumbler of wine, and raised it high above her head.

"It is my great pleasure," she declaimed. "To announce the winner of our all-star wit and brilliance competition. Our panel of distinguished judges have been debating the matter most earnestly for the last twenty-five minutes, and have come to the unanimous decision that this year's title of Miss Twenty-two Woodchurch Avenue shall be awarded to Mrs Eileen Forbes. . . ." Once again the glass was deposited with ceremony in front of the unfortunate girl, who seemed visibly to flinch. Rosamund caught her breath: once more Eileen was to be shown up as a spoil-sport, and ridiculous as well, for no one could have failed to notice that in wit and brilliance she had lagged far behind her sister.

Rosamund glanced sideways at Geoffrey to see if he, too, saw unkindness in Lindy's gesture. But no. He was beaming kindly, unsuspiciously on both sisters, and he joined in warmly and good-humouredly when Lindy burst into frenetic clapping at the end of her speech.

Was it all meant kindly, just a bit of fun? Rosamund

could not tell. For Eileen's sake, she tried to lead the conversation back to the subject of the book department.

"It must be very interesting, helping people to choose books," she began, addressing herself to the discomfited girl; but Lindy interrupted:

"Yes, it suits Eileen down to the ground!" she declared. "A good, steady, respectable job, with a pension at the end of it—she's the Careers Mistress' Dream, our Eileen! I'm *not*, I'm afraid, I'm more like her Nightmare! Security has never appealed to me, somehow, and as for the idea of a *pension* . . . !"

Geoffrey laughed at the horror she put into the word.

"So what do you do, then?" he enquired. "Do you always extract an assurance from prospective employers that the job is not pensionable, and that they will sack you without warning almost at once?"

"More or less! How well you understand me, Geoff!" Lindy seemed delighted. "Actually, I'm doing something even madder than that at the moment—I'm trying free-lance fabric-printing. Terribly precarious, as you can imagine. It's a good thing *one* of us is doing something sensible and steady, isn't it?"

She shot an approving glance at Eileen, and try as she would, Rosamund could not be sure that she saw traces of scorn or pity in it. Was she misjudging Lindy after all?

She was filled by the same doubts all over again when, later on, Lindy unearthed a guitar from the clutter and sat by the open French window, gently plucking chords under the cloudy summer night. Her fingers wandered for a while, erratically, among her rich mental repertoire of assorted tunes, and finally settled for "Oh Careless Love", which she began to sing softly as she played.

"Come on, join in, folks!" she urged, after the first verse; and first Geoffrey and then Rosamund did so. But not Eileen. Was she sulking, or disapproving, or was she just hopeless at singing? If she was, then Lindy would know it—once more Eileen was to appear at a disadvantage.

Lindy had a lovely voice. It rose into the summer darkness clear and true as a nightingale; or was it, rather, like a bird of prey?

CHAPTER IV

That evening was the beginning; and at that stage Rosamund wasn't being a jealous wife at all. Nothing had happened, yet, to make her think of Lindy as a rival, and the empty, frustrated feelings that assailed her as they returned home, long after midnight, had nothing to do with jealousy. It was just that she felt done out of the after-party gossip that she and Geoffrey usually enjoyed as they went to bed, laughing about this or that person or incident, comparing notes about the pleasure or boredom they had derived from the evening.

But Rosamund learned tonight that comparing notes is only a pleasure if your notes have been pretty well identical with those of the other person. It wasn't comparing at all, really; it was just a companionable gloating over sameness, and all the more enjoyable for that. What fun they could have been having tonight, for instance, talking over Lindy's affectations—her flamboyance—her veiled spite towards her sister—if only Geoffrey had seen her behaviour in this light too. But his innocent delight in the whole evening's entertainment was like a bright, blank wall—it offered no door, no chink, through which any sort of conversation could start. Or so it seemed to Rosamund. It wasn't conversation to exchange remarks like: "Yes, wasn't it marvellous?" or "Yes, she must be a very vital sort of person" or "Yes, it *will* be fun having people like that next door instead of the dreary old Sowerbys."

It had been more fun, actually, having the Sowerbys, Rosamund thought rebelliously. The gloomy, disagreeable Sowerbys, with their eternal complaining and bickering, and their neat rows of moribund seedlings put in every spring by Mr Sowerby against the advice of Mrs Sowerby. Almost any evening it had been possible to start an amusing conversation with: "Do you know what the Sowerbys are rowing about *now?*"—and thus, amid laugh-

24

ter, to savour the success and happiness of their own marriage in contrast to this miserable pair.

As she lay wide awake that first night, staring through the window at the waning summer moon, Rosamund felt a terrible nostalgic longing for the Sowerbys. For Mr Sowerby's boots, which he was for ever failing to wipe when he came in from the garden; for Mrs Sowerby's relations, whom he was for ever failing to be polite to. . . . What fun it had all been! Like a long, catastrophic serial story, suddenly cut off in its prime to make way for one of those dreadful *happy* stories, where nobody has any proper troubles, and there is even a Pekinese with a red bow. . . . Rosamund could see the creature as the centre-piece of a full-page illustration, clutched in the arms of a vapid, jolly girl. . . .

"The sister was nice, too," came Geoffrey's voice suddenly—she had thought he was asleep. "Much quieter, of course, than Lindy. More reserved. But nice."

"Yes, they're both very nice," agreed Rosamund, like a parrot, and was glad that Geoffrey couldn't see her face. I *hate* nice people, she was thinking crossly. I like nasty people. Interesting, disagreeable, nasty people that you can really talk about—laugh about. People, she might have added, who make me feel superior; but this was no time of night to be embarking on such a disturbing train of thought; so Rosamund closed her eyes against the waning radiance of the night, and fell asleep.

It was Monday morning when she saw Lindy again; a still, golden, heat-wave morning, perfect for the washing, or for writing letters in the garden, or mending, or indeed for just lying there, staring up through green branches at the hot, still sky. And this last was exactly what Lindy was doing. As soon as she saw Rosamund across the fence, adjusting her clothes line, she called out: "Rosie! You *can't* work on a day like this! Nobody could! It shouldn't be allowed. Come over and have an iced coffee at once!"

Her voice was friendly, genuinely welcoming. She really *does* like me! thought Rosamund, in some surprise —she had somehow assumed that her secret feelings of hostility the other night must be mutual. So she set down her basket of washing, forgot her momentary

annoyance at being called "Rosie", and stepped over the
low fence into the next garden.

The iced coffee was delicious, in long thin glasses, pur-
plish dark, with great fluffy balls of cream bobbing tantalis-
ingly to the surface as you stirred. *I* would never go to
all this trouble just for the woman next door, thought
Rosamund remorsefully; so to make amends for this, as
well as for all her unkind thoughts of the last forty-eight
hours, she exerted herself to be appreciative.

Besides, she was curious. She wanted to know all about
these two sisters—their lives, their troubles, their past, their
future. Almost instinctively, she set herself to be just
as charming and friendly as is necessary to have another
soul lay its secrets at your feet—and was astonished at how
quickly and easily it worked. Could it be that Lindy was
doing exactly the same thing?

"Poor Eileen's a funny girl, in some ways," explained
Lindy, slowly stirring her coffee, now cloudy with dissolv-
ing cream. "She's very pretty and charming and all that.
And clever, too. Eileen's much cleverer than I am really,
you know. Always did better at school—that sort of thing.
You'd think, wouldn't you, that with all that she'd be
all set for a really happy and successful life."

"And isn't she?" asked Rosamund, unashamedly inquisitive now that she had Lindy safely launched on her
confidences.

"No. It's a funny thing, but whatever she embarks on,
it somehow seems to—well—fizzle out. It's as if she lacked
the—what is it? The energy?—zest?—whatever it is that
gets one's life swinging along on its own momentum.
Everything that happens to her, she seems to have to *make*
it happen, laboriously. And then, to keep it going, she has
to work at it all the time. Her marriage was like that, you
know. It was dreadful to watch her toiling away at it!"

"What happened, then?" asked Rosamund comfortably, sure, now, that the story would go on whether she
prompted or not. "I know you told me it broke up . . .?"

"Yes. And he was a nice boy, too. It was a shame."
Lindy stared into the dazzle of greens and golds in front
of her, slowly twirling the glass in her fingers. "If *I* had
a husband"—she suddenly went off at a tangent—"If *I*
had a husband, and had to go out to work as well, I'd
do everything in my power to make him feel not guilty

about it, wouldn't you? For instance, I'd somehow manage to get home in time to have everything looking nice for him, and myself all ready to welcome him. Not fussing over the cooking and the housework, but relaxed—at leisure—the way a man likes to find his wife. As if she'd been doing nothing all day but making herself beautiful for him!"

"Well—it's a pretty tall order!" Rosamund couldn't help protesting. "I mean—with a full time job! Especially for a girl as young as your sister must have been when she got married."

"Oh, Eileen's not as young as all that!" Lindy assured her, rather sharply. "That childlike manner of hers is deceptive. She was old enough, anyway—or so I should have thought—to have realised what it was she was doing to her marriage. Evening after evening Basil would come in to find his wife scuttling madly about, making beds, peeling potatoes, cleaning grates—for all the world as if she was doing it on purpose to make him feel guilty. That's the one fatal thing for any woman—to make a man feel guilty. It kills everything. But Eileen just couldn't see it."

"She may have *seen* it all right," objected Rosamund, rather hotly. "But what on earth could she do? I mean— I've never had to work full time myself since I've been married, but I'm quite sure it must be terribly hard work. You'd just be compelled to do housework all the evening— and if your husband wouldn't help, then he'd just have to feel guilty, *I'd* say—and serve him right! I think he *should* help, in a case like that."

Lindy shook her head, smiling with an air of rather irritating—it seemed to Rosamund—incredulity.

"I'm really rather intrigued by the way married women are always up in arms on this question of working wives," she mused, smiling as if to herself. "Whether they themselves work or whether they don't, the first thing that most of them think of is how 'hard' it is for the wife! As if they were determined to seize on the question as a stick to beat their husbands with—an outlet for their unconscious hostility. 'It's not *fair!*' they say —like children in a nursery! *I* wouldn't worry whether it was 'fair' or not. I'd want the man I loved to come home to what every man really wants—absolute leisure, tranquillity and comfort; and the feeling that his wife has nothing to do but to attend to him. He doesn't *want* to know that his wife has been working all day, and she shouldn't thrust the fact under his nose, the way most of them do."

"It's all very well!"—began Rosamund indignantly on Eileen's behalf—and indeed on the behalf of all married women—and then she stopped. How could you argue with someone so untried, so unaware of the practical problems involved; someone so adept, too, in the use of weapon-words like "guilt" and "unconscious hostility"—the inflated armchair jargon with which it is possible to batter other people's practical problems into silence?

"Sometimes," Lindy went on reminiscing, "Eileen would try to do as I advised. She'd tear madly home, running all the way, to have time to put on a pretty dress and look relaxed by the time Basil got back. Relaxed! It would have been funny if it hadn't been so pathetic. You felt all the time that the strain of being relaxed was killing her! No wonder poor Basil packed it in. I tried once or twice to show her how it could really be done—how it was possible to give a man a pleasant, leisurely meal at the end of his day's work: but she just turned sulky. She's never liked being in the wrong."

All Rosamund's dislike of Lindy was flooding back. She set down her glass with the feeling that she could not swallow another mouthful of the black, evil fluid. She could see with lurid clarity the gay little parties that Lindy must have laid on for her sister's discomfiture. The candles, the laughter, the informality; with Lindy tranquil and triumphant at the heart of it all, trusting to Basil's masculine obtuseness to prevent him realising that this kind of meal *did* need a lot of preparation, that Lindy, a single woman, had been able to devote to it time which Eileen would have had to be devoting to sweeping floors and washing her husband's shirts. And Eileen could have done nothing to enlighten him. Loyalty—timidity—pride—all these would have silenced any protest she might have felt inclined to make. And if, by any chance, she *had* protested, then Lindy would still have won, and even more triumphantly. For what more unloveable and unlovely spectacle can there be than that of a wife whining that *she* could be kind and charming too, if only this that and the other. For whatever this that and the other may materially be, spiritually they are, of necessity, three vicious blows at the husband's self-esteem. Lindy, unmarried and inexperienced, knew it all: used it all with practised skill, like an artist working in an alien medium that he has managed to make utterly his own.

A low snarl within a few inches of her made Rosamund almost leap out of her chair. It was as if some avenging spirit had been reading her uncharitable thoughts, and was about to strike. And even when her startled wits had taken in that her accuser was only a very small, very suspicious Pekinese, she still wasn't quite sure that her first instinct had been unfounded. Those bulbous, inscrutable eyes mirrored who knew what ancient, forgotten wisdom in their uncanny depths? Did the dog somehow know—sense—smell—that here was an enemy to his mistress?

Hastily Rosamund smiled and held out her hand. "Good doggie!" she pleaded sycophantically, and tried to pat the rigid, hostile little body. But her insincere and incompetent blandishments were of no avail. The dog retreated a couple of paces, and set up a shrill, impassioned yapping, his flattened, ugly face contorted with what looked like more than human rage.

"Shang Low, you silly! Be quiet!" admonished Lindy admiringly, and with no effect whatsoever. "It's because he doesn't know you, you see," she explained lazily above the din. "He's a very good guard dog really, although he's so tiny. Pekes are."

The last two words, simple generalisation though they were, seemed to Rosamund to be spoken in an oddly self-satisfied way, as though Lindy felt that she, personally, had supervised the three thousand years of intensive breeding that had gone to produce Shang Low and his self-righteous fury. Rosamund felt her irritation overflowing, quite out of proportion to its trifling provocation.

"I like cats better!" she said, quite sharply, and was shocked at the naked rudeness of her tone. But Lindy only smiled, wholly unruffled.

"I'm sure you do," she said easily. "I could have guessed that as soon as I saw you."

The words were spoken lightly, but Rosamund could feel in them a sting, sharp and deliberate, though as yet quite unacknowledged. But before she could think of any retort, or even decide whether retort was indeed appropriate, they were once again interrupted. This time it was Mr Dawson from the other next-door garden. He stood, secateurs in hand, beaming admiringly from among his great cream-coloured roses, his admiration seeming to embrace indiscriminately the little yapping dog, Lindy's brown gleaming legs in their becoming striped shorts, and the tall, cool glasses on the tray. All the glories of a suburban summer morning thus spread before his kindly gaze, he seemed to feel the need to join in, to make himself a part of it all. So "Good morning!" he called out, over the fence. "Lovely morning, isn't it? Nice little dog you've got there."

"A dreadful, noisy little dog, if you ask me," laughed Lindy, turning towards the newcomer, confident of being contradicted. "I do hope you don't mind him?"

"Oh no, not a bit. Not a bit." Mr Dawson leaned further over the fence. "I like dogs. Used to have a dog ourselves ——Oh, for years. He was nearly sixteen when he died, poor old chap. But the wife thought we'd better not start all over again with a puppy. Not with the kiddies both grown up by that time, and left home. *You* know."

"What a shame!" said Lindy, with rather more sympathy than it seemed to Rosamund that the subject called for. It was not clear if her condolence referred to the death of the old dog, or to the misfortune of having a wife who didn't want a new puppy, or to the sadness of having all your children grown up and away. "Do come over and join us," Lindy continued hospitably. "We're having iced coffee—I'm sure that's just what you need after all that gardening."

Mr Dawson seemed enchanted by this prospect. He abandoned his secateurs and climbed with clumsy alacrity over the intervening fence; and in practically no time at all, it seemed to Rosamund, Lindy had managed to welcome him charmingly, to produce a third comfortable chair without seeming to go and fetch it, and to set before them three fresh sparkling glasses of iced coffee, topped with yet more cream. What a larder the girl must keep! thought Rosamund, with unwilling admiration. Fancy being able casually to produce mounds of whipped cream for anyone who happened to drop in unexpectedly in the middle of Monday morning!

Mr Dawson was looking cherished, happy. He leaned back in his chair and sipped his coffee, his bronzed, balding head and amiable features gleaming with warmth and contentment as the sun mounted towards its zenith, and Lindy, wide-eyed with interest and sympathy, steered him with consummate skill through the story of his life; encouraging him to linger on such episodes as redounded to his own modest credit, and to pass over those which did not. Once again Rosamund found herself forced reluctantly into admiration. She had always flattered herself that *she* was a good listener, a sympathetic confidante. But now, listening to Lindy, she had to own herself utterly worsted in this field. In ten years of living nearly next door to the Dawsons, of meeting and chatting with them, she had never learned a fraction of what Lindy was learning now, in less than an hour's conversation. Had never known that Mr Dawson had always longed for a daughter as well as his two sons; that he had wished, as a boy, to go in for farming, or market-gardening, or something like that, but had given in to his parents' importunate passion for security and gone into insurance; how sometimes, to this day, he regretted his cowardice. "Particularly on a day like this," he confided, closing his eyes luxuriously against the glory of the noonday. "When I think of the hay just cut in the meadows, and the larks far up in the still blue sky, and the hedges white with—er—well, with that white stuff. . . ."

"I suppose you *could* move to the country now, if you wanted to?" interposed Rosamund sympathetically. "Now that you've retired, I mean——"

Lindy was showing more sense. Lindy was keeping quiet. Rosamund realised in the very instant of speaking that she was saying absolutely the wrong thing; was shattering poor Mr Dawson's precarious little dream.

"Oh. Ah. Well——" Mr Dawson heaved himself into a less comfortable position in his chair as he sought a way to extricate himself from this disconcerting proposition; to bolster up his nostalgic vision against this onslaught of real possibilities. "Oh, well, you know, at my time of life. . . . And then our friends, it would mean leaving all our friends, you know; the wife wouldn't like that. And there's the Women's Guild, too, remember. The wife's a great one for the Women's Guild. Very keen. Very keen indeed. Did you know, they're going to do a play in the autumn? Lady Windermere's Fan. And the wife's to be Lady Windermere herself! That's the main part, you know. The most important part in the play!"

The pride in his voice was unmistakable. Lindy looked up quickly.

"How funny," she said. "I'd have thought that that was a part for a younger woman. Though I'm sure Mrs Dawson will do it very nicely," she amended smoothly. "Won't you have a little more coffee?"

Mr Dawson was about to reply when a faint stir of movement from next door, scarcely audible to other ears, alerted him, brought him bold upright in his chair.

"The wife's back!" he announced, getting hastily to his feet. "Think I ought to be popping back. Give her a hand, you know—duty calls. Thank you for a most delightful interlude, Miss—er——?"

"Lindy. *Please* call me Lindy," protested his hostess, getting up also. "And do call over again, whenever you can—and bring Mrs Dawson too, of course. I do so want to get to know my neighbours."

She smiled delightfully. Nothing could have been more charming, more unaffectedly friendly, than her manner. You felt that she really did want to meet Mrs Dawson, was really looking forward to it.

And yet, the very moment Mr Dawson's back door banged shut behind him—as if it were a cue for which she had been waiting—Lindy's expression changed completely. She resumed her seat, edging closer to Rosamund as she did so, and burst into low, impassioned speech:

"What a shame!" she ejaculated softly. "What a wicked shame! Poor fellow! Has it always been like that?"

"Has what always been like what?" asked Rosamund blankly. "Do you mean the Dawsons?" She was quite baffled by this outburst following so incongruously on Lindy's pleasant farewell speeches to Mr Dawson a few seconds ago.

"Of course I mean the Dawsons. *Mrs* Dawson, that is. She must be an absolute bitch. You know her?"

"Yes, of course I know her," said Rosamund, bristling a little. "And she's not a bitch at all. She—"

"But she must be! Surely you can see it? Didn't you see how scared he was? The moment he knew she was in— and he must have been absolutely on tenterhooks listening, because I didn't hear a thing—the moment he heard her, he leapt up as if he had been stung! Didn't you notice?"

"But it wasn't like that at all—you don't understand," protested Rosamund. "They're a very happy couple. He came over here because he was at a loose end while she was out shopping, and as soon as she came back he went home again. It was as simple as that. Besides, I expect he wanted to see what she'd brought for lunch. He does most of the cooking for the two of them, you know, now that he's retired."

"Well—I think that's dreadful, too," insisted Lindy. "After a lifetime of hard work, you'd think a man might be allowed to have a bit of a rest when he retires. These women who seem to regard retirement as an excuse to turn a man into a domestic servant—"

"But she doesn't! It isn't like that at all. He loves cooking—it's his hobby. He hunts up all sorts of exotic recipes to try out, and is terribly proud of himself when they turn out well. And so is she—she goes round boasting about how clever he is. *I* think it's sweet. And very wise of her to encourage him. Some women would be complaining about having a man messing about in their kitchen."

"I don't doubt it. But the trouble with you, Rosie, is that you see it all from the woman's point of view," said Lindy, with maddening condescension. "From the *married* woman's point of view, that is to say. But I sometimes think that we single women are more in touch with the way a man really feels. We aren't blinded by the way we *want* him to feel, the way so many married women are. It affects their whole outlook, on everything. You see, the average wife not only wants her own husband to have the feelings she has chosen for him; she wants husbands in general to have those feelings, too. It makes her feel safe. Look how anxious *you* are, for instance, to prove that Mr Dawson just loves having to cook lunch; and that it is sheer devotion to his wife that makes him jump like a scalded cat when he hears her come in. And how *quietly* she comes in, too,—didn't you notice—no slamming the front door or anything? As if she was

hoping to catch him out at something. . . . Oh, I'm sorry,
Rosie. She must be a friend of yours—I mustn't go on like
this about her. Let's talk about something else." She
smiled at Rosamund, charmingly: "What shall I do with
this garden? What do you advise? I want to put in something that will really brighten it up next summer. Do you
think tulips?"

"*Yes!*" said Rosamund, between her teeth, unappeased
by the chance of subject. "Lots and lots of tulips. You
couldn't do better."

Lindy glanced at her quickly, a little puzzled by her
vehemence. She couldn't know, of course, that tulips
were Geoffrey's and Rosamund's pet hates. Nasty, stiff,
artificial looking monstrosities, Geoffrey had always
said; might as well be made of plastic. And they'd
agreed, with gloriously abandoned prejudice, that only
stiff, disagreeable sorts of people went in for tulips; people with no real heart.

"Tulips would be perfect," Rosamund repeated encour-
agingly. "Have rows and rows of tulips in every bed. And
in the front as well."

CHAPTER V

"Have you seen the fork, Rosamund?" asked Geoffrey
one Saturday afternoon in late August. "I want to help
Lindy with a bit of digging."

Rosamund did not reply for a second: she was thinking.
Not about where the fork might be, for she knew very well
that it was in its usual place in the toolshed. And Geoffrey
must know this too—he wasn't asking for information at
all, she realised. Rather he was asking for some sort of
backing—a reassurance from Rosamund that she didn't
mind his spending so much of his weekends over at
Lindy's. It was as if by getting Rosamund to tell him
where the fork was, he was in some way bringing her into
this plan for re-designing Lindy's garden: making the
whole project into a threesome, not just him and Lindy.

"It's in the toolshed," said Rosamund, following his train of feeling exactly. "I'll get it for you." As she carried it across the tired, yellowing August grass, she wondered whether to feel touched or uneasy at the look of relief on his face. It was nice of him to want to feel assured that she wasn't feeling jealous or left out: but how insulting that he should think she might be!

As if I would! Rosamund handed him the fork with a bright smile, and then turned savagely on that tiny cowering corner of her soul which might perhaps be tempted to feel bitter at the sight of her husband's arms and shoulders bronzed and rippling with muscles in the service of another woman.

She—Rosamund—jealous? Never would she so degrade herself as to feel—let alone show—such an emotion. So she went smiling back to her solitary tasks of tying and staking overblown plants, of clipping the ragged edges of the lawn. Between the blades of the shears she could feel that summer was already gone; the grass was long and quiescent; the surge and spring of growth was over. The shadows lengthened as she worked, and the enfeebled sun, already touched with autumn, slanted weakly down, scarcely warming her shoulders as she worked. Across the fence she could hear the rhythmic plunging of the fork into rich earth; could hear Lindy's voice rising and falling; laughter, and Geoffrey's voice, happy and amused. Did he sound as happy as that at home? Presently she went indoors, and could hear it no more.

Geoffrey came back soon after six, sunburnt, glowing, with his boots covered in mud. At the sight of his happy face Rosamund realised in one spiteful unheralded flash of insight that, in his mind, Lindy must be getting the credit for a sense of well-being that in fact came merely from hard physical exercise.

So, as an unjealous wife should, she smiled, and made no comment on the traces of mud spreading through the kitchen . . . through the hall . . . up the stairs . . . into the bathroom . . . down the stairs . . . into the sitting room. *She'd* expect me to nag him about it, Rosamund reflected truculently, but I just won't, that'll show her!

So she made no complaints, and showed herself full of interest in Geoffrey's afternoon activities as they sat talking afterwards.

". . . about five hundred weight of clay, I should think!
Really, I'm not exaggerating! And we hadn't a barrow,
so I had to carry every scrap of it in buckets. Gosh, what
my back will be like tomorrow . . . !"

But he wasn't complaining, Rosamund well knew. He
was boasting; glorying in the hard physical work of
which men are most of the time deprived. Why don't *I*
want the garden dug up? thought Rosamund crossly; it
seemed so unfair that Lindy should have this advantage,
on top of so many others, simply because Rosamund
liked their garden the way it already was: a lawn, a tangle of
hardy, colourful perennials, and a single glorious blossom
tree.

"What's she going to do with it, anyway?" she asked
hopefully, remembering the tulips. Perhaps Lindy had
in mind something absolutely frightful; something that
Rosamund and Geoffrey would be able to lean out of the
landing window and criticise every summer for years and
years.

"Well—she was suggesting a little paved area in the
centre, to catch the sun, surrounded by masses and
masses of tulips. Rather a striking idea, don't you think?"

"Striking, perhaps. But—*Tulips*!" Rosamund laughed,
and put into the word all the happy, united prejudices they
had shared over the years. She waited for Geoffrey's answering laugh, which should have been immediate, and
rich with shared memories.

"Well—I don't see why not," he said uneasily. "I
mean, the way she's planning it—she's thinking of having
all different sorts all massed together—all sorts of colours.
Scarlets, and yellows, and flame colour, and those huge,
very dark blackberry-coloured ones."

This was not Geoffrey speaking, Rosamund knew. He
was not naturally very imaginative, or given to vivid
description. These were Lindy's words. It was Lindy who
had poured all these colours into his head in glorious
headlong profusion—Lindy who had led him to this be-
trayal of his and Rosamund's joint hatred of tulips.

With half her mind, Rosamund knew how petty and
ridiculous it all was. *Tulips*! What a thing to be bothering
about! With the other half, she was aware of black
treachery.

"It sounds gorgeous," she heard herself saying brightly.

"Lindy's always full of marvellous ideas. Let's ask her to supper this evening, shall we?"

Even as she spoke, Rosamund knew exactly what her motive was: she was terrified that Geoffrey had been going to make exactly this suggestion himself. By thus forestalling him, her pride was saved. She need never know now that he *had* been going to suggest it. For all she need ever know, he might have been feeling that he'd already seen quite enough of Lindy for one weekend.

He looked pleased and touched. "Lovely idea. What a good girl you are, Rosamund." He kissed her gratefully, and she felt the kiss like the imprint of a message in code. A message thanking her for not making a jealous scene; for being nice about the Other Woman; for not being as other wives are. A flattering message, in its way, but one which bound her to a course of action from which there was no returning.

But I'll invite someone else as well, she decided defensively: a married couple perhaps would be the best idea. The mere presence of another wife would give her a feeling of moral support, and—delicious thought, this—the other wife *might,* if provoked, behave towards Lindy in all the ways in which Rosamund would have loved to behave. Sooner or later *someone* will have to be uncivilised, she reflected, but if I play my cards carefully it won't have to be me.

Horrified to discover the depths of scheming to which she could sink, Rosamund hurried to the telephone, and rang up the first likely pair she could think of.

Even at such short notice, the Pursers turned out to be able and delighted to come, and they arrived only a few minutes after Lindy herself, both wearing that air of escaped prisoners which some parents develop over the years and never lose—an air of guilty, precarious enjoyment of a brief spell outside. William Purser was a serious, balding, young-old person, who was devoting himself, rather early in life, to being disappointed in his son. His wife Norah was serious, too, but her seriousness was masked by the almost permanent smile which lit up her little anxious, ravaged face. She was disappointed in their son too, but, unlike her husband, she made it her job to make the best of it; a wearing occupation, which left her

tense and nervy, whereas her husband was at least able
to relax in his depths of settled gloom.

"And how's Peter?" was the first thing Norah asked, when
they were all settled round the table in front of bowls of
Rosamund's onion soup. "Still doing nicely at school?"

"Not bad," said Rosamund, wishing that there was a
little more to boast about in Peter's unruffled but sadly me-
diocre performance in the educational rat-race—if race it
could be called which seemed to leave the whole lot of
them free to lean on their bicycles arguing outside the
front gate for the whole of every weekend. "We think he's
getting pretty lazy, actually," she added kindly, knowing that Norah's "How's Peter?" was really asked in
the hope of hearing that Peter was already showing signs
of being as tiresome as her Ned. Norah would then be
able to assure herself—and her despondent husband—that
all boys were like that at sometime or another, it was
just a phase. . . .

Sure enough, Norah's fixed smile widened into a spark
of real hope. "Is he? Is he really? They do get like that,
you know, at about that age" (she flashed an almost
imperceptible glance at her unresponsive partner). "That's
just when Ned began to be so difficult, at about sixteen.
He'd done brilliantly till then, really brilliantly . . . I sometimes think that perhaps this is something they *need*, you
know, these bright boys. To knock around a bit. . . . Find
their feet."

Her husband glanced up from his soup balefully.

"I don't call it 'finding his feet' to hang about the house,
out of a job, lying in bed till midday. . . ."

"Oh, William, but that's not fair! It's only the last
couple of weeks that Ned's been unemployed. He——"

"The last *five* weeks," contradicted Ned's father remorselessly. "And before that in April. And that packing
thing over Christmas was only part time. If that boy's
done as much as ten weeks' solid work since he left school,
I'll . . ."

The uneasy wrangle over facts and dates went on, and
Rosamund watched Lindy drinking it in, silently, with
relish, like a second, extra nourishing, bowl of soup. She
was thinking, you could see, some more of her favourite
sort of thoughts about wives and their inadequacies. Dev-
astating reflections about the way they messed up the re-

lationships of their husbands and their sons were probably maturing inside that sleek black head, and Rosamund determined to interrupt them.

"Half the battle is to get them out of the house," she broke in cheerfully. "Peter's gone off cycling with a friend this weekend, and it's such a relief! All the way to Canterbury and back, with practically no money and nothing to eat! But they don't seem to mind."

With some annoyance she heard the pride in her own voice. She had never meant to be one of those mothers who are for ever boasting about the physical achievements of their sons, the hardships endured by them. But somehow it was irresistible, far more so than boasting about their academic successes. And evidently Norah found it so too, for she instantly leaped into the competition.

"Oh *yes!*" she exclaimed. "Ned had six weeks in France last year with literally no money at all! He slept under bridges—got himself washing up jobs in return for meals—"

"And was back in a fortnight," interposed William. "Owing about seven pounds to an American family who took pity on him, and the whole of his fare home. And he didn't go penniless. Norah, you're talking absolute rubbish. He had ten pounds in travellers' cheques, and——"

"Well, after all, he was barely nineteen," began Norah defensively. "Lots of boys——"

"And their Peter is only sixteen!" interrupted William, with an exaggeratedly approving glance towards Rosamund. "Now, there's a lad with guts for you! Setting off to cycle a hundred miles just for the joy of it! If Ned had ever done such a thing, ever, in his whole life. . ."

Rosamund murmured some sort of deprecating protest, but she couldn't help being pleased. She knew, of course, that Peter's virtues were only being used as a stick with which to beat the nefarious Ned: she knew, too, that the approving glance had fallen on her rather than on Geoffrey, who was surely equally entitled to it, because William wanted to highlight, by contrast, Norah's lack of maternal skills. A congratulatory glance at Geoffrey might have set people thinking that fathers have something to do with their sons' shortcomings, too.

"When a boy is lucky enough to have a really sensible

mother," he hammered on, in case anyone had somehow succeeded in missing the point. "A mother who doesn't spoil and cosset him, why, then he naturally grows up courageous and enterprising, full of zest for this sort of venture. . . ."

A thumping and a clattering in the hall . . . the slam of the front door . . . the dining room door thudding open, and there in front of them stood Peter, his straw-coloured hair falling even further than usual into his eyes, and his mouth open in unmannerly horror at the sight of his parents' guests.

"Oh, we got fed up," he explained, in answer to his mother's dismayed queries. "We got tired, before we even got to Gravesend. It seemed a bit pointless."

Rosamund tried to hide her total dismay. Not only was her recent ill-gotten prestige as the mother of an enterprising son laid in ruins, but her whole weekend—her lovely Peter-less weekend—lay shattered about her like a trayful of smashed china—you couldn't even begin to count up the losses, to sort out what was still intact, in that first moment of shock. And Peter just kept standing there, eying the table (covered with appetising food but surrounded by horrifying guests) with just the sort of fixed, apprehensive look with which a dog regards a dinner that has been given to him too hot.

"Well, go and find yourself something to eat in the kitchen," urged Rosamund inhospitably, and with the grim brightness appropriate to an embattled mother who is also trying to be a gracious hostess. "Go on," she repeated, the grimness fast overwhelming the graciousness as Peter went on standing in the doorway.

"Walker's here," he observed. He seemed to expect his mother to understand that it was this fact which was keeping him rooted to this irritating and inconvenient spot, and to expect her to do something about it. Rosamund leaned back a little in her chair to peer round the door. There, sure enough, was Walker, the dreadful speechless companion of Peter's cycle rides. Speechless, that is to say, in Rosamund's presence: she supposed that he must speak sometimes, or how could all these outings be arranged, let alone cancelled. Whether the boy's silence was due to shyness or to deep thought it was hard to tell, and even harder to care. Rosamund stared at the two of them with growing irritation. Why did Peter have to look so *short,* she thought crossly, on top of everything else? Rather small for his age in the first place, he was now standing, as if deliberately, with his head slumped into his shoulders and his shoulders slumped into his spine as he leaned against the edge of the half open door. His left hand fiddled uneasily with the doorknob behind him as he waited limply for his mother to make some decision which would somehow heave the two of them into some other room.

"Well, take Walker with you, and find him something to eat," said Rosamund, struggling to let calm reasonableness predominate in her tone, while maintaining an undercurrent of sufficient savagery to ensure that they would actually go. "Go on. Look in the refrigerator. Go *on!*"

"O.K. C'mon." Peter at last abandoned his stance by the door and disappeared in the direction of the kitchen. For one terrible moment Rosamund thought that Walker hadn't moved, wasn't going to move. But it was all right; he too had vanished. Too much relieved at their disappearance to call them back to shut the door—*anything* rather than have either of them back, for any reason whatsoever—Rosamund surreptitiously shut the door herself under cover of fetching a dish from the sideboard. At last she was able to turn her attention back to her guests, who by now were happily discussing the flavour of octopus as served in Sicily. Lindy was happy, that is to say, and so were the two men. Norah seemed less happy, as Lindy had just that moment managed to elicit from her, in the most public manner possible, that in twenty-two years she had never once attempted to cook octopus for her husband in spite of knowing that it was his very favourite dish. William was looking almost aggressively smug and understood.

Rosamund was half listening to the talk, half to the sounds through the wall from the kitchen. The expert, almost telepathic ear of motherhood—or is it just housewifehood?—could ascertain through nine inches of brick and plaster that the boys were only having bread and jam and cornflakes, and that in a very few minutes they would be finished. Would Walker go then, or what? Please, God, prayed Rosamund, as she distributed stewed pears and cream, Don't let Walker stay the night. Oh, dear God, don't let him!

CHAPTER VI

But Walker *did* stay the night. When Rosamund stumbled sleepily into the kitchen in her dressing-gown the next morning there he was, neatly and completely dressed, sitting at the kitchen table expectantly. On Sunday morning, too, she protested to herself in silent horror, closing her eyes for a second in the dim hope that perhaps when she opened them he would have disappeared. On Sunday morning, at barely half past eight! Just when she had been planning to make a pot of tea for herself and Geoffrey and to go back to bed with it for hours and hours. And if this wretched boy *must* stay for the night, why couldn't he at least lounge about in bed till midday, wasting the whole morning, like other boys? She opened her eyes, without much hope, and sure enough, there he still was, looking at her. Sooner or later somebody must say something, and clearly it wasn't going to be him.

"Hullo," she said, as unchillingly as she could. "I'm just going to make some tea. Would you like some?"

"Yes, please."

He could say things like that all right. It was an exaggeration to claim that he didn't talk at all, Rosamund reminded herself contritely. She filled the kettle, lit the gas, terribly conscious all the time of the ghastly unoccupiedness of her unwanted guest. Did he *have* to just sit there like that, doing nothing?

"Wouldn't you like the paper?" she suggested brightly. "I expect it's arrived by now. It'll be out on the step."

"No, thank you," said Walker, swivelling his polite, expressionless gaze from the corner of the ceiling to his hostess' face. Then, as if this degree of activity was all that anyone could possibly demand of him, he proceeded to wait, politely expectant, for Rosamund to say something else.

"The kettle won't be long now," she remarked desperately; and then, when Walker made no reply, she went on: "Wouldn't you like to make yourself some toast? We're always disgracefully late on Sundays—we shan't be having breakfast for ages."

"No, it's all right, thank you," said Walker. "I'd rather wait."

And wait you shall, thought Rosamund grimly, swilling out the teapot with boiling water. Convention forbade her venting her annoyance on the silent figure, whose total lack of occupation seemed to be positively boring into her back as she bent over the sink; and so, instead, her thoughts turned wrathfully towards her son, the irresponsible author of it all, sleeping peacefully upstairs. What did he mean by bringing in this dreadful silent friend and dumping him on Rosamund to entertain, like a cat bringing in a dead bird? Let *him* get up, make toast, have his Sunday morning spoilt. It was *his* visitor.

She went to the door.

"Peter!" she yelled up the stairs; and then, going up to the landing: "Peter! Wake up! Come on down!"

Silence, of course. She went into her son's room and shook him violently by the shoulder.

"Wake up, Peter! Your friend Walker is up, and waiting for his breakfast. Do go down and look after him, for goodness' sake!"

"What a fuss!" Peter sat up, and rubbed his eyes. Then the full unreasonableness of the demand broke over him.

"But it's *Sunday*!" he protested. "I don't have to get up at this hour on Sunday!"

"You have to *this* Sunday," said Rosamund with relish. "Because you have a visitor. I keep telling you, he's down there in the kitchen waiting for his breakfast. You can't just leave him there."

"But why not?" Peter's greenish flecked eyes were round with mingled sleepiness and surprise. "Walker doesn't mind."

Rosamund realised with a shock that this was perfectly true. Walker *didn't* mind. He probably had not experienced one moment's embarrassment during that (to her) ghastly interlude in the kitchen. *She* was the one who minded. She was the one who was made uneasy by a guest who was doing nothing, saying nothing. But young people—or was it just boys?—simply did not feel these sorts of emotions. They spoke if they had something to say; moved if they had something to do. If they hadn't, they might be bored, but it wouldn't occur to them to be embarrassed. This was an adult—or was it a feminine?—or even just an old-fashioned?—state of mind.

"You have an obsession about visitors, Mummy," said Peter tolerantly, as if he had been following her train of thought exactly. "But it's all right. Honestly. Walker's a marvellous chap that way, he never expects anyone to fuss over him."

This was putting it mildly, Rosamund thought, as the daunting picture of someone trying to fuss over Walker flashed for a moment through her mind. But anyway, there seemed no point in arguing any more; Peter's head was firmly under the blankets again, and downstairs she could hear the kettle dancing and shrieking its protests at her neglect, boiling its heart out, no doubt, under the interested, untroubled gaze of Walker.

Lindy arrived just in time for their eleven o'clock breakfast. That is to say, she dropped in at eleven o'clock, and Rosamund—as had been her policy ever since she became aware of the attraction between her husband and Lindy—had begged—pressed—her to stay. The nicer, the more hospitable, she was to Lindy, the less anyone could possibly regard her as a jealous wife: that was her reasoning. And not being regarded as something was half way to not *being* it, thought Rosamund uneasily, as she smilingly set a plate of bacon and mushrooms before Lindy. Perhaps, if I go on smiling at her, inviting her in, laughing at her jokes, pushing her and Geoffrey together —perhaps all this un-jealous behaviour rolled all together into one great heavy ball may some day roll back and crush my actual jealousy to death? Or perhaps (more practical thought, this), perhaps Geoffrey will get sick and tired of her if I keep stuffing her down his throat? Which of these is my motive really? And to think it all looks like being tolerant and good-natured! Is this always the secret of the tolerant, broad-minded wife?

"Won't you have some more coffee, Lindy?" she urged warmly. "It's nice and strong, this time, the way you like it."

Lindy passed her cup with a murmur of thanks and a

smile. For a second the two smiles met in mid air, like
warring aircraft; and then both fled, as if for cover, to
Geoffrey. Both women spoke to him at once:

"Do you think we should phone your mother about what
time we're coming?" said Rosamund; and, "Do tell me
more about that funny couple last night," said Lindy. "The
Pursers"; and there could be no doubt that her remark
was much the most interesting as well as her smile the
most brilliant. So it was only natural—as well as polite
—that Geoffrey should answer her rather than his wife.

"Well, Purser is a metallurgist," he began, obligingly
but naïvely. "A Manchester man . . ." as if those were the
sort of things that anyone could possibly want to know
when they asked to hear "more" about a person.

"—And he hasn't always been so gloomy," supplemented
Rosamund, smiling affectionately at her husband's in-
ability to get quickly to grips with this sort of conversation. "They really do worry terribly about that boy of
theirs. Though from everything you read in the papers,
he doesn't seem so specially much worse than the others."

"I don't think there's any harm in *any* of them," said
Lindy vehemently. "I think it's all the fault of—"

Was she really going to say "society"? Was she actually
going to voice such a platitude, and in Geoffrey's hearing?
Rosamund hugged herself. Surely no man, however in-
fatuated, would go on thinking highly of a woman's wit
and intelligence if she could produce as her own idea so
monstrous a cliché?

"The mothers," finished Lindy suavely. "I don't think
the fathers come into it any more—not now. Their wives
don't let them."

"How so?" Geoffrey seemed intrigued. Disputation, of a
gentle kind, usually pleased him, particularly at weekends. It
made him feel young and leisured, back in his student days.

"Well—look at the Pursers, for instance," said Lindy
—Rosamund, but not Geoffrey, had seen from the start
that the sociological generalisation about mothers was
simply a highbrow introduction to saying something nasty
about Norah Purser—"Look at the way she was all the time
identifying with the boy at the expense of her husband.
That was what was hurting him so. Not the fact that his
son was delinquent, but that the delinquency was being used by his own wife to set up a barrier between

the three of them. Her and the boy on one side: Father on the other. Don't you see?"

There was wisdom in Lindy's words; and injustice, too. Rosamund leaped on the injustice; consciously she magnified it, made it seem the main subject of the debate. Even as she did so, she was shocked at her own skill.

"*I* think the boot was quite on the other foot," she declared hotly. "I thought William was being really horrid to Norah. He was deliberately showing her up, in public, as having brought the boy up badly. As if *he* had had nothing to do with it at all!"

"As he probably hadn't!" retorted Lindy. "That's exactly what I'm saying. Just think what it must be like from the man's point of view (she carefully did not look at Geoffrey as she said this; she seemed to be talking to Rosamund alone). Just think: he pays, and pays, and pays for eighteen—twenty—years; and what does he get in return? Can you wonder that he sometimes looks at his sullen, unresponsive son, and thinks to himself: There goes ten thousand pounds of my money; seven thousand evenings which I might have enjoyed with my friends; a thousand peaceful, pleasant weekends. . . ."

Geoffrey was laughing, as if Lindy had made a delicious joke. So Rosamund tried to make her protest sound like a delicious joke, too.

"But, hang it all, Lindy, anybody could calculate like that about anything! I could look at *my* son and think: There goes fifty thousand hours of washing-up, and——"

"Implying that you wash up for eight hours a day!" interrupted Lindy lightly. "It sounds more like running a hotel than bringing up a son!"

Everybody laughed again. It was Lindy who had been witty enough to make them laugh; Lindy who had won the argument, too, simply by getting her beastly sums right. If she had got them right? Rosamund was still trying to multiply one and half three hundred and sixty fives by sixteen in her head when she heard Lindy proclaiming, still lightly: "And of course, when it's an only son, the situation is even worse. . . . Ned *is* their only one, isn't he?" She added the question quickly, and with great innocence, as if to show, a second too late, that she had quite forgotten that Geoffrey and Rosamund had an only son.

"No, he isn't!" said Rosamund triumphantly, and as

if somehow scoring a point. "They've got a girl, too, she's about fifteen. But we don't hear so much about Sarah because she isn't any trouble. Except for having a crush on T. S. Eliot and keeping writing herself imaginary letters from him. But that's what I'd *call* not being any trouble. So quiet."

Geoffrey began to laugh; but stopped almost at once; for though Lindy was smiling, her smile held the faintest trace of embarrassment, as if Rosamund had said something not in the best of taste.

"It *does* seem amusing, I know," she said, with an air of much more unruffled tolerance than seemed to Rosamund at all necessary. "From the point of view of an outsider, that is. But, you know, this schoolgirl crush business—it's not quite so amusing at close range. I should know, after bringing up a younger sister. And it gets less amusing still if it goes on too long."

Nothing more. No explanation. No opening for anyone to ask further questions. With sudden fury, Rosamund realised that Lindy's sister was to be left for evermore just faintly shadowed by this nebulous hint of some intangible degree of abnormality. But before her anger could show in her face, before it could twist her pleasant, un-jealous smile into something quite strange, there was an interruption. For at that moment the slam of the front door crashed through the house, shaking the crockery on the shelves, jerking a new expression onto everyone's face. Then came the sound of two bicycles thumping down the steps; the creaking clash of the front gate; and then quietness, like a wind, swept back into the house.

"There goes our ten thousand pounds' worth," commented Geoffrey good-humouredly. "Our thousand quiet weekends. Our——"

"And the Walker boy with them, I trust!" said Rosamund, recovering her temper. "Oh, it was so *ghastly* this morning, Lindy, you can't imagine . . . !" and she began to relate—quite amusingly, she flattered herself —the story of her encounter with Walker in the kitchen.

At the end of the recital Lindy as well as Geoffrey laughed.

"You do make it sound so funny, Rosie!" she declared. "Doesn't she, Geoff?"

Rosamund should have been disarmed by the compliment; but it happened that in that very moment she noticed why it was that she so hated Lindy's habit of using these abbreviations of both their names. It was because it seemed to imply that she, Lindy, was on more intimate terms with each of them than either were with each other. How stilted and distant "Geoffrey" was going to sound if Rosamund were to bring his name into her next remark —which of course she wasn't. Indeed, she wasn't going to have a chance, because Lindy was continuing:

"It makes a good story, Rosie, I grant you; but when you come to think of it, what dreadful manners the boy must have! I suppose his mother is an ardent believer in child psychology—not frustrating them, and all that?"

"Not that I know of," said Rosamund, rather tartly. "That sort of thing hasn't got nearly so much to do with how you bring up your children as outsiders think it has. People who've never had children always talk as if merely not believing in child psychology automatically made you into a good disciplinarian. It's much more complicated than that. And anyway, most of these frightful fifteen and sixteen year olds, they *were* well brought up in the sense you mean. I've watched them with my own eyes evolving out of the most charming, well-behaved little boys. Peter was a little marvel at seven, you know. Passing round cakes at tea parties. Standing up for old ladies in buses. The lot."

Lindy looked incredulous. So, to her dismay, did Geoffrey. Was she really remembering it all wrong, as mothers were said to do? Or——?

"Oh, I daresay discipline is more difficult as they get older," Lindy was saying. "I'm not denying it. But it just goes to prove what I was saying before: At just the point when the father could and should be the major influence, disciplinary and otherwise—at just that point the mother begins to cut him off from his son. To put up the barriers. So he can no longer get discipline, or anything else, across to the boy."

Geoffrey was looking horribly thoughtful. Rosamund frantically tried to think of some come-back that would be kind, polite, good-humoured, and would knock Lindy sideways.

But all she could think of was a rather dull change in the conversation, but one that at least would put Lindy and her carefully aimed insights out of the picture for the moment.

"Don't you think we ought to phone your mother?" she asked Geoffrey, once again. "And let her know that we're coming this afternoon?"

"Oh. Ah. Of course." Geoffrey looked uneasy, and turned to Lindy. "You won't mind, will you, Lindy? I shan't be able to start on the crazy paving this afternoon after all. I'd forgotten this was the Sunday for Mother's."

"Oh, but it needn't be!" Rosamund fell over herself to release her husband for Lindy's exclusive use this sunny afternoon. "Next Sunday will do just as well. She's not specially expecting us. . . ."

"Oh, but Geoff, you mustn't upset your plans because of me! . . ." For a moment the battle of self-effacement ricocheted between the two women, both of them talking together, and the sound was like the whirring of wings in the small sunny kitchen. And Lindy won.

"Well, actually," she admitted. "If you *did* decide to put off going till next weekend, I could drive you there. I'll have the poor old car in running order at last—at least I trust so. How'd that be?"

She looked brightly, generously, from one to the other of them; and even Rosamund couldn't see undercurrents of malice in the suggestion. For Lindy, of course, couldn't possibly know of her and Geoffrey's little prejudice against cars; couldn't know how much they enjoyed the walk from the station, right through the little sunlit town where Geoffrey's mother lived, past the churchyard, and up the long, tree-lined road that was very nearly country, and where the hawthorns still bloomed in the spring: where every step, every gateway, reminded Geoffrey of his boyhood; might, at any moment, inspire him to some anecdote, some memory, which even now, after all these years, could still show him to his wife in a new, an excitingly different, light. Half the point of going to Mother's was this walk. They wouldn't give it up for anything.

"Well, that *is* an idea!" said Geoffrey enthusiastically. "Save our old bones for once, eh, Rosamund? Ashdene can't be much more than an hour away by car, do you think, Lindy . . . ?" He and Lindy fell to animated discussion about routes, and Rosamund was left smiling. "I wish she was dead!" she said to herself, clearly and dis-

tinctly, as she smiled. And it was only long afterwards,
when the time had come for her to subject every tiny
shred of memory to a panic-stricken scrutiny, that she
noticed that this was the very first time that the thought
of Lindy's death had come to her in so many words.

CHAPTER VII

"You really should learn to drive, Geoff! You'd be good."
Lindy had been explaining, with the greatest of good-
humour, exactly why it was that she had changed gear
on this hill but not on the previous one. Why couldn't she
lose her temper, like other drivers, thought Rosamund
crossly. Why must she remain bright and serene in the
midst of this chaos of Sunday traffic inching its way out
of London, and at the same time answer fully and sympathetically all Geoffrey's eager, amateurish questions?
For after all these years of anti-car prejudice, Geoffrey
had overnight become as excited as a schoolboy over the
idea of learning to drive. Excited as schoolboys were supposed to be, that is to say, thought Rosamund wryly, from
her corner of the back seat. Not like the two schoolboys
she had left sitting side by side on the kitchen table, slowly
finishing an entire tin of rock cakes while they discussed
the gloomy future of the world: just like a pair of vultures,
Rosamund thought, hovering arrogantly over the entire
decaying universe as if it were their rightful prey. Still,
they'd probably be better once they got out on their bicycles; and with any luck they wouldn't be back for hours
and hours. Why, it might even happen that Peter stayed the
night with the other boy for once, instead of the other way
round.
Rosamund realised that her spirits were rising, though
goodness knew why, with her husband and Lindy talking
cars non-stop in the front seat, and the whole Sunday trip
to Mother's spoilt, perhaps for ever. Perhaps Geoffrey
would always want to come like this, in Lindy's car? Perhaps he would want to buy a car of their own? And this

afternoon would have been so specially lovely for walking. Already, within a week, the sad, tattered, end-of-summer look was gone from the countryside, and the still, blue September skies were back. But you could not feel the stillness from the car, nor smell the stubble fields. The golden, gentle sunshine became a mere metallic beating of hotness through the car roof, and you couldn't even talk. That is to say, Rosamund couldn't talk, not from this solitary corner.

She had chosen it, of course. Of her own accord she had urged Geoffrey to sit in front with Lindy, to help her with the map-reading, she'd said. As always, her status of odd one out in their trio was of her own deliberate choosing, and thus could not be felt as a humiliation. But it *looked* like a humiliation. Rosamund had been shocked, as they set out, to find how much she was hoping that the neighbours weren't peering out from the Sunday somnolence behind their curtains; weren't noticing how Lindy and Geoffrey were paired off in the front of the car, for all the world like a married couple, with the spinster sister of one of them lurking at the back.

But probably the neighbours were already talking, anyway. Every time Geoffrey went over to help Lindy in her garden, a dozen upstairs windows must be taking note, setting one Saturday afternoon beside another, drawing gleeful conclusions. If only there was some way of *telling* them that she, Rosamund, wasn't the neglected wife at all; that, on the contrary, it was all just a beautiful family friendship, with Rosamund herself freely encouraging all these visits and exchanges. She would have liked to label her husband, when he went over to Lindy's, with a huge gaudy card saying: "A Present From Rosamund", because that's what it amounted to, and it would be so nice if the neighbours could know.

Nice, too, if her mother-in-law could know, she now realised, as they turned in to the short gravel entrance of Geoffrey's old home; welcoming as always with its warm brick, its square, unpretentious windows, and the jasmine round the front door.

Wondering briefly at her own disproportionate anxiety not to be seen on the back seat, Rosamund scrambled ungracefully to the ground almost before the car had stopped, went round to the front, and stood smiling in at the window while Geoffrey and Lindy discussed arrangements for the return journey. Lindy was being admirably tactful about not expecting to be invited in to meet the elder Mrs Fielding. She wanted to explore the town, she declared, and the neighbouring countryside; to examine the old tombs in the churchyards. . . . This and that. . . . She would call back for them at about seven—and brushing aside their protests and expressions of gratitude, she drove quickly away, leaving them to walk up to the front door together, just as always.

Except that it wasn't as always, and perhaps would never be again.

Jessie, Mrs Fielding's old servant, answered the door to them, neat and invulnerable in her cap and apron, her kind old face lighting up with discreet pleasure at the sight of them. Jessie knew how to "keep her place" with such exquisite skill and dignity that you quite forgot that her "place" no longer really existed in the world today: the niche which she had occupied for fifty years had to all intents and purposes been swamped and obliterated long ago by the swirling tide of the twentieth century. And yet she occupied it still, like an old, smooth stone, impervious to battering waves, immobile among the shifting sands.

Her mistress seemed much more modern, although several years older. Mrs Fielding looked up briskly from the Journal of Hellenic Studies as they entered her book-lined drawing-room, gathered her papers together, and at once entered into eager conversation, mainly with Rosamund.

"You've just come at the right time!" she declared. "I've just finished the draft of a letter I'm going to send them about this Henriksen man's findings. 'Findings' indeed! It's 'Guessings', as always in this Linear B racket . . . ! Wait a moment. . . . I know I had it. . . . Just here somewhere. . . ." She perched her gold-rimmed glasses precariously back onto her nose as she shuffled through the tangle of documents. "Ah, here we are——" She drew out a sheet of closely-written, tissue-thin typing paper, and handed it to Rosamund. "I'd like you to look through it, dear, if you will, and give me your opinion. Have I expressed myself too strongly, do you think?"

She had, of course. She always did. But all the same, the

curt, uncompromising phrases, the fire of genuine indignation, gave a special flavour of her effusions, which perhaps explained why the editors of these so learned journals did occasionally print them. It was odd, really, that she should choose Rosamund as her confidante on these highly specialised matters—Rosamund, who knew not one word of Greek, and whose initial knowledge of Knossos and all appertaining thereto did not extend beyond a sketchy recollection of the story of Theseus and the Minotaur. But after all these years of regular visits to her mother-in-law she knew a great deal more about it all now; and what she lacked in scholarship she made up for by an affectionate sensitivity towards the way the old lady was likely to feel towards a given incomprehensible inscription or scholarly statement or whatever it might be. And, dominating all else, was the enormous admiration she felt for a woman who had been able, after the age of sixty, to set herself to re-learn a language she had not set eyes on since she was in the fifth form at school, and within the next fifteen years to reach such a standard of proficiency in the whole subject as to be able to squabble, however wrong-headedly, with the recognised experts in the field.

Geoffrey, Rosamund was well aware, found it all rather boring; but he was an affectionate and dutiful son and was only too delighted that Rosamund was able to get on so well with his rather thorny and opinionated mother, and apparently to share her interests. So he roamed contentedly enough about the room, looking at a book here, a magazine there; and Rosamund, sitting in consultation with her mother-in-law over the letter, was aware of his slow, familiar movements as a part of the peculiar peace of this room, this house. In her mind, the decipherment of Linear B would be for ever simply a part of this gentle, shining drawing room, with its small fire crackling, its fire-irons bright gold with daily rubbing, and every mahogany surface polished, speckless; gleaming from Jessie's lifelong care.

At four o'clock exactly, Jessie knocked discreetly on the door, and wheeled in the trolley of tea-things. "Thank you, Madam," she murmured, as she set the final cup in position beside her mistress and turned to go: and "Thank you, Jessie," replied Mrs Fielding, clearly and formally. It occurred to Rosamund that within this rigid, formalised relationship there flowed, perhaps, a warmth, a close-ness, far deeper and more binding than many that flourish so demonstratively in the outside world.

The Palace of Minos was forthwith abandoned for the time being. Mrs Fielding's upbringing made talking shop at mealtimes out of the question: so while she poured out from the silver teapot, and handed round the lovely, delicate survivors of the old Rockingham tea serv-ice, the talk became general; that is to say, it concentrated on News about the Family. They got Peter over first, and quickly. Rosamund always found it rather a strain to think of something both new and vaguely creditable to say about him every fortnight or so; and as soon as possible she got the old lady switched onto Cousin Etty and the Boys—the Boys being by now middle aged and elderly men, in and out of hospital, and with daughters getting mar-ried, that sort of thing. It so happened that Rosamund had never met any of that branch of the family; and so Cousin Etty and the Boys had joined Linear B in her imagination as the gentle concomitants to an endless vista of tranquil old-world teatimes. They had become as one with the hand-made lace cloth; with the silver sugar-basin and sugar-tongs; with the home-made jam in cut glass dishes; everything softly shining; everything perfect of its kind.

Before they left, Rosamund found time to slip into the kitchen and talk to Jessie for a few minutes. As always on Sunday evenings, Jessie was using her free time after tea to write a letter to one or other of her nieces in Australia. Already, for her, it was a cosy winter's night. She had the curtains closely drawn against the September sunset, a thick green cloth spread over the scrubbed wooden table, and in the background the Aga cooker mur-mured softly, as the old kitchen range had done long ago. This was Jessie's sitting room, and she would have chosen no other. Every pot and pan, every cup and plate, stood dry and shining in its appointed place; every working sur-face lay scrubbed and clean, ready and inviting for to-morrow's tasks. On the top shelf of the dresser stood photographs of all Jessie's nieces' weddings, together with the shells and ornaments they had sent her from the other side of the world; and in the drawers below were col-lected a lifetime's store of magazines, newspaper cuttings, old letters; and also more utilitarian oddments like string, stamps and sewing materials, any one of which she could have laid her hands on in the dark, even one of the newspaper cuttings.

For a second, Rosamund stood in the doorway, gazing at the familiar scene, a vision of changeless, absolute security, which had no counterpart anywhere else in her experience. Only Jessie's glasses, familiar sight though they were, created a very slightly jarring note. She only wore them for this special task, just once a week, and so they still looked a little like fancy dress on her; just as the very ordinary paraphernalia of letter writing—ink, writing-pad, blotting paper—managed to look, in this setting, a little bit like stage properties: not quite a part of the whole.

But in the next moment Jessie had noticed her visitor in the doorway, had removed the glasses, and looked like herself again. They went through the tiny, unchanging ritual of Jessie's making a move as if to stand up respectfully, and Rosamund hastily urging her to remain seated, sitting down herself at the opposite side of the table, and asking after the niece who had most recently had something happen to her. This time, it was the one whose husband had recently been put on night shift, which unsettled his stomach.

"A raw beaten-up egg in milk, that's what he should have, first thing when he gets in of a morning," said Jessie firmly, and with an absolute certainty which must surely carry its healing sureness across eight thousand miles of troubled lands and heaving waters. "I'm just telling her, she should keep him to that for a couple—three—weeks, and then work him along to a nice brown egg lightly boiled. . . . They can get lovely eggs out there, you know, Miss Rosamund. Real, big, new-laid eggs."

"Miss Rosamund" was perhaps not the most suitable title for a married woman of eighteen years' standing; but long, long ago Jessie had decided, quietly, and entirely on her own, after months of uneasily not addressing Rosamund at all, that "Madam" simply couldn't be paired with "Master Geoffrey"; that an address of manifest incorrectness was the only solution; and "Miss Rosamund" it had been ever since.

"See here," continued Jessie, sliding a stiff, glittering square of cardboard from an envelope. "She's sent me my birthday present ever so early this year. I suppose the posts and all, she wanted to be sure. . . . Pretty, isn't it?"

She handed Rosamund a rather over-ornate calendar, covered with blue and silver flowers interwoven with blue and silver good wishes and worthy sentiments.

"But I wouldn't use it," went on Jessie carefully. "I'm going to put it away all nice, perhaps it'll come in another time. I wouldn't want to change my old one, that's the truth. . . ."

"Change what?" Geoffrey had at that moment entered the kitchen, and was beaming on the two of them: "What are you two girls gossiping about now?"

Although he seemed to be laughing at them, Rosamund knew that he loved the way she fitted into his old home—fitted better, in a way, than he did himself: loved to find her chattering like this with old Jessie in the kitchen.

"It's Jessie's calendar," she explained. "Her niece has just sent her a new one, but she'd rather go on just fitting the new set of dates into the dear old cottage one, wouldn't you, Jessie?"

They all glanced up at the wall, where the painted plywood shape of a cottage hung, with painted curtains to its windows, painted hollyhocks along its base, and its front door designed as a gap in which date and month could be inserted. It had hung there, over the table, ever since Rosamund could remember, and the little verse, painted in ornate, faded letters under the eaves, was by now so familiar that she was hardly aware of it any more. But this evening, her attention freshly drawn to it, she read it consciously and attentively for the first time in years:

> "Lord, make it mine
>   To feel, amid the city's jar
> That there abides a Peace of Thine
>   Man did not make, and cannot mar."

Jessie's calendar. Jessie's prayer. In the course of her quiet, ordered life, lived apparently in such unchanging calm, had even she felt at times the tumult, the longing for peace? Had there been times, over the long years, when unguessed at tempests had torn and battered at her secret soul; when turmoils and despairs unspoken had hammered

behind her starched apron and her neat black dress? Had
she at those moments read and re-read the lines on her
little wooden cottage, and found the peace they promised?

With a rush of love, Rosamund was aware of Geoffrey
reading the words too, carefully and attentively as she
was herself, without mockery or condescension. A tender,
happy smile played about his mouth: he, too, must be
thinking these same thoughts about the faithful old servant of his childhood.

He spoke softly:

"It reminds one of Lindy, doesn't it? *She's* peaceful in
that way. No matter what's going on around her—
traffic—parties—noise—she still remains at peace, tranquil within herself."

Rosamund could have torn the calendar from the wall
and flung it at him. She could have thrown herself on the
floor in a passion of rage and weeping. She could, after
recovering the power of speech, have bombarded him
with furious argument. Lindy *isn't* tranquil, she could
have screamed: she's a bundle of nerves; she's all tensed
up, all the time, with the strain of pretending to be calm
and gay. I know it. . . . I sense it. . . .

But instead she smiled, keeping her eyes fixed on the
aging, multicoloured letters, which now seemed to her to
be written in fresh, bright blood.

"Yes, there aren't many people like that, are there?"
she replied evenly: and a moment later they heard Lindy's
car crunching on the gravel. It was time for her to drive
them home.

CHAPTER VIII

Even as a surgeon, trained over the long years to almost
superhuman skill and sensitivity, may examine the patient beneath his hands for the almost imperceptible symptoms of a deadly disease, so did Rosamund, all her faculties
sharpened by fury, examine Lindy's face, her posture, the

whole of her demeanour, for tiny, miniscule symptoms of some huge, corroding tension, or at least of common or garden impatience.

For Lindy had explained, in arranging to call for them at seven, that she wanted to be home by eight; and yet here she was, at twenty past seven, still smilingly and charmingly listening to Mrs Fielding's impassioned defence of Evans and all his works in the Palace of Minos. As kindly and cleverly as ever Rosamund herself could have done, she was encouraging the old lady with tactful interventions, of a sort which indicated her interest without betraying her ignorance. Never once did Lindy's eyes flicker towards the clock; never for one second did she let her interest seem to flag, as a preliminary to ending the conversation. How relaxed she looked, damn her, one arm resting lightly along the arm of the chair, the other lying loosely in her lap. Rosamund watched, sharp-eyed as a weasel, for those white, well-manicured fingers to start fiddling with something; picking at the braid on the armchair, perhaps; pleating up a bus ticket; anything at all to indicate some tiny degree of inner tension.

But it was no use. And in the end it was Geoffrey who had to remind them that time was getting on.

"Oh, what a shame! Yes—I suppose we *should* be going really. . . . It's been so interesting, Mrs Fielding, I really don't know how to tear myself away. . . ."

So it was on the cordial farewells between his mother and Lindy that Geoffrey beamed this time, as he usually did on his mother and Rosamund.

"You must come again, my dear, I would be so pleased if you would!" exclaimed Mrs Fielding to Lindy, as she showed them all to the door. "Do bring her again, Geoffrey, won't you?"

"It's a case of *her* bringing *us* at the moment," laughed Geoffrey. "She's introduced a car into our lives, you know, Mother, and we're really quite bitten! Next thing you'll know, we'll be driving up to your door in our own Rolls and taking you for drives. How would you like that?"

"It would depend how you drove," said his mother cautiously. "I've never felt you were one of Nature's mechanical geniuses, Geoffrey. Particularly since the time you told me I was only imagining that noise in the geyser, and it blew up the same night!"

"Oh, Mother, I didn't say you were *imagining* it! I said——"

"Well, never mind, dear," interrupted Mrs Fielding annoyingly. "You haven't even got a car yet, have you, so there's no need to argue. Goodbye, dears. See you all again soon, I hope. When you can next spare the time."

She stood waving in the lighted doorway while Lindy edged and backed them into position, and then swept the car slowly, gracefully, out into the dusky road. Down under the great trees, under the gathering hosts of stars, and out into the streams of cars in the main road.

The traffic was even worse now than it had been this afternoon. People must have seized on this last warm basking sunshine of the season to swarm in thousands to the coast; and now here they all were swarming back, tired, irritable, scowling narrow-eyed at the bumper just ahead. As the slow crawl came at last to a total stop some of them began hooting, with sharp, poignant hopelessness, to somebody or something; perhaps to unhearing Hermes, god of travellers, long vanished from the earth, and who can blame him?

And what god can *I* pray to, wondered Rosamund, running her mind over such classical deities as she could remember. Which was the goddess whose special task it was to watch over bad-tempered wives cooped up in a five-foot box with Another Woman of angelic good-humour, of unruffled calm? Oh, dear goddess, whoever you are, prayed Rosamund, show me how to make her annoyed and upset without it being in the least bit my fault. If you would just do that for me, I think I really would sacrifice a sheep to you, or whatever it was you wanted. At least, I would if I thought it would fit into my oven, but I'm sure it wouldn't, it's bad enough with the turkey at Christmas. Besides, the butcher would think I was mad, asking for a whole sheep.... It's no wonder the Olympians have deserted the earth, with everything so complicated. ...

"Get a move on, sister!" yelled the man in the car behind them, sticking his head through his window. He sounded very cross and unreasonable, and pinched his hooter spitefully as he spoke. Lindy leaned out and threw him an enchanting smile:

"So sorry, pal," she called. "But I can't do a thing. We're all in the same boat, aren't we?"

The scowl left the man's face. He grinned apologetically. Geoffrey looked at Lindy with delight.

"There can't be another driver on the whole road who could have achieved that!" he declared admiringly. "This is the most rotten luck for you, I must say," he went on, gesturing at the glittering shambles of standing cars in every direction. "I'm terribly sorry we've let you in for this. There isn't a hope of being back by eight, I'm afraid, it's practically that now. Was it something very important?"

"Oh, only our party," said Lindy lightly. "I was going to do the food and things, but it doesn't matter. I daresay everyone'll be late, anyway. *You* will for one, that's quite certain! And so will Rosie!"

"I didn't know we'd been asked." Rosamund could hear that Geoffrey was smiling in the darkness. "It's the first I've heard of it."

"Oh, well, you know me!" said Lindy. "I only thought of it this morning, and I just rang everyone up straight away. I meant to ask you when we started out this afternoon, but it went right out of my head. So I'm asking you now. Will you come to my party, on Sunday the 13th of September, at 8.0 p.m. or as soon after as the hostess happens to turn up? No. On second thoughts, let's start it on the dot! Eight p.m. *prompt* is on the invitation card now!"

She took her hands off the wheel, reached into the glove compartment and drew out a small square bottle and three plastic mugs.

"Vodka," she explained. "To get the party going! Will you divide it out, Geoff? There's only a teeny drop, but still, we might as well enjoy ourselves while we sit here. Nothing's going to move for hours yet. So here goes, boys and girls! The party's begun!"

You could, if you didn't mind how nagging and mean-spirited you sounded, have pointed out to Lindy that she shouldn't drink while she was driving. But by the time it had been divided into three, the vodka filled less than half an inch at the bottom of each mug; that amount couldn't possibly affect anyone, least of all a driver as confident as Lindy. And anyway, Rosamund knew very well that rather than make such a wet-blanketing sort of protest in her husband's hearing, she would willingly have sat by and watched Lindy drinking a pint of the stuff: yes, and would have accepted her fate in the ensuing pile-up without so much as an "I told you so!"

I'm just a criminal; a plain criminal! thought Rosamund, shocked at herself as she realised that, just to save her own selfish pride, she would without a qualm have condemned half a dozen people to death or disablement.

But it was silly to agonise like this: Lindy *wasn't* drinking a pint of vodka. And all that giggling with Geoffrey didn't mean she was drunk at all; it was simply that she had thrown out the daring proposal that they should invite the irascible driver of the car behind to join them in this little celebration.

"Poor man, I feel so sorry for him, all alone in his car, eaten up with impatience, and no one to swear at! I'm sure he'd love it—and it *is* a party, isn't it?"

"But, my dear Lindy, suppose it all starts moving suddenly, then where will he be? I'm sure we could all be arrested, or something!" Geoffrey sounded as if he was half laughing, half shocked, and wholly intrigued.

"Oh, nonsense! I tell you, nothing's going to move for hours yet. I always think that these real, outsize jams could be made a wonderful social occasion, if only people would be a bit more enterprising. You could have debates, lectures, parties. . . ."

In the end, of course, they didn't invite the man in the car behind: but they went on giggling about the possibility of it, like school-children, till Rosamund could have screamed. And her distress was not only for the here-and now situation. She also knew, with that deadly stir of intuition that clutches at the spirit, that this, for Lindy and Geoffrey, was going to be one of those memories. One of those times that they could look back on even after forty years, and still say: "You remember that man in the car . . . ?" Every time Vodka might be mentioned from now on, Geoffrey's glance would meet Lindy's in swift, mutual recollection. The memories he shared with Rosamund were already, perhaps, becoming shadowy, tiresome; something to remember with an effort, like a cousin's birthday. . . .

It was well after nine when they reached home, and as

the car drew up, Rosamund saw lights streaming from every one of the windows of Lindy's house. There was the sound of music, voices; the party had evidently begun without her.

"See?" the errant hostess exclaimed happily. "There was no need to fuss! There never is. Parties just run themselves, if the hostess will only relax!"

The remark could hardly have been aimed at Rosamund, who had not given any sort of a party, relaxed or otherwise, since Lindy had come to live here. Nevertheless, the words seemed somehow to have the quality of missiles, flung at random into the darkness at the back of the car: carelessly, as much as to say: With any luck some bit of this will hit and hurt her; but if not, why, there's nothing lost, it was no bother. No trouble at all, dear; a pleasure. . . .

"Come on in—I'm longing to go to my own party!" cried Lindy excitedly, as they left the car. "Both of you come along, at once."

"Well, just give us a few minutes," said Geoffrey. "I want to get changed. . . ."

"Yes. And I must see if Peter's in, too," added Rosamund, though she couldn't think why she must. It was a breathing space she wanted: a little bit of time in her own home, away from Lindy, away from the sight of her and Geoffrey together.

"O.K. Don't be long," Lindy called. She had reached her own front door by now, and across the two gardens Rosamund saw her feeling for her key in her handbag.

But before she could find it the front door was flung open with a great blaze of light, and Rosamund could see Eileen framed in the brilliance; could hear her voice, low and frantic:

"Lindy! How *could* you! Why have you been so long? How *could* you leave me to cope with everything on my own? And *this* time of all times! You *knew* that Basil might be coming!"

CHAPTER IX

So *that* was the secret of all this relaxed hostess business! Lindy was simply leaving her sister to do everything, while claiming credit herself for superhuman light-heartedness and calm. If only Geoffrey was listening . . . was taking it in!

But no. As ill luck would have it, he had hurried straight indoors, and hadn't heard a word of the significant exchange on the other side of the fence. Rosamund followed him into the house slowly, trying to think of a way of reporting the incident without sounding catty. How it did cramp one's style, this not being a jealous wife! How much less interesting it made one, too; for the anecdote, catty or not, would at least have been amusing and stimulating—could have triggered off the kind of conversation that Geoffrey and she had once enjoyed nearly all the time. As it was, there seemed nothing to talk about while they got ready for the party except whether to lock the back door; as to which Rosamund found herself disagreeing with Geoffrey simply for the sake of something to say. Never, ever had it been like this with them before. . . .

The party was in full swing when they arrived, and looking swiftly round Rosamund calculated that every single one of their neighbours must have been invited. How well Lindy had managed to get to know everyone in the three months she had lived here! Better than Rosamund had done in all the past ten years, to judge by all these familiar faces gathered together. Familiar in a sense, that is: in another sense quite unfamiliar, for faces that you are accustomed to meeting under hats or over garden walls look queer indoors, like the postman without his uniform. In a way, it was easier to talk to the total strangers; the bearded artistic men and the un-house-wife-looking women who must have come out of Lindy's former life. Letting herself be pushed unresisting by the surging movements of the crowd, Rosamund presently found herself wedged tête a tête in a corner with a wiry,

pale young man who looked like a poet, but who said
that he was a Shell Shelder, or something that sounded
like that: indeed, for all Rosamund knew, there might
really *be* such a job; anyway, you couldn't go *on* asking
him to repeat it, any more than you could ask him to go
on repeating his name, also lost in the surrounding din.

Gradually, as her ears became accustomed to the noise,
she gathered that he was talking to her about modern
marriage. Before much longer, she found that she could
actually hear everything he was saying, and no longer
had to reply with such smiles and platitudes as would be
equally appropriate whether he was describing the faith-
lessness of his wife or the Darby and Joan happiness of
his aged parents.

It was neither, and the platitudes couldn't have been
in the least appropriate, but perhaps he hadn't heard
them:

"The wonderful thing about just *living* with a girl,"
he was saying, "is the privacy and the dignity of it. People aren't watching you all the time, the way they are when
you're married, to see how you're making out. I mean,
an affair is expected to break up, so people don't get any
kick out of watching for it to happen. And they don't
think it's against the rules for you to go out separately
sometimes, or for you to have different tastes, different
friends. Stepping out of an affair into marriage is like
stepping out of a civilised state into a goldfish bowl. Wher-
ever you look, whichever way you turn, there are great
eyes staring at you, hugely magnified, watching to see
how you match up to the Perfect Husband. Or Perfect
Wife, of course: it's just as frightful for her, too. I'm not
saying it isn't."

Rosamund laughed. "It sounds as if you have a heavy
concentration of in-laws," she said. "And your wife, too.
Are you both members of big, devoted families?"

"On the contrary, we are both orphans. Were, I
should say. My wife and I are separated."

"Oh! I'm sorry!" Rosamund felt some embarrassment, but the young man hastened to dispel it, in his
rather disconcerting way.

"Don't be silly! You don't have to apologise. Hang it
all, *I* brought up the subject. I wouldn't have, would I, if
I'd wanted it tactfully avoided?"

"No, that's true," said Rosamund. "It's just that one is rather brought up to . . ."

"There you are! That's another thing!" interrupted her engagingly indignant companion. "The way everyone feels they've got to be so bloody *tactful* about marriage, as if it was a fatal disease, or a deformity, or something. They stare, and they point, and they whisper, but they won't *talk* to you about it. Nobody asks you how it's going, whether you're enjoying it, that sort of thing, the way they would if it was a new job, or a trip abroad, or any other exciting new venture in life. Your friends all get so remote and evasive, it's like being stranded on a desert island; just you and this young woman. Not being a character in a film, I just couldn't take it."

"Well, you've said you don't like people to be tactful, so I won't be," said Rosamund. "I must say, it does sound to me as if you must have given up rather soon. All that kind of thing—what you've been describing—subsides pretty soon, you know. People soon get tired of watching and speculating, and then you get forty or fifty years of peace and quiet. If that's what you want."

"You don't really believe that, do you? People never get tired of watching and speculating. Not ever. All you really mean is that you find compensation in all the chances *you* get to watch and criticise in *your* turn. I don't mean you in particular," he added hastily, suddenly looking very young. "I mean 'one'."

"*Now* who's being tactful?" smiled Rosamund. "You might very well mean 'me in particular', because I'm sure I'm terribly like that. No, what I mean is, people are curious at first, naturally, because they don't know what this new personality, the-pair-of-you, is going to be like. As soon as they *do* know, they stop being inquisitive. It's like getting to know any new person."

"Well, in the first place, I resent suddenly being counted as half of a new personality when I've spent twenty-six years being the whole of an old one, and enjoying it thoroughly, thank you very much! And in any case, none of this answers my second objection: the way people boycott the subject of your married state as a topic of conversation. And *that* doesn't change. I daresay *you've* been married quite a few years, but if I were to ask you, quite simply and conversationally, how you'd enjoyed it, you'd evade the question in horror, wouldn't you?"

"Yes, I would," said Rosamund; and began to consider why she would. Loyalty? Cowardice?—Or simply that it was none of this young man's business?

The last thought must have shown in her face, for he laughed a little defensively:

"There you are, you see? Whereas if I'd asked you how you'd enjoyed living in this neighbourhood all these years—and *that's* none of my business, either—then you'd tell me quite happily, and we could have an interesting discussion about it. And then I'd tell you where *I* lived, and you could ask how I felt about it, and it would all be quite interesting, probably. . . ."

"Well, where *do* you live?" Rosamund was beginning obligingly, when Lindy suddenly appeared through the line of shoulders and backs cutting off their corner from the rest of the room.

"Oh, *there* you are, Basil!" she exclaimed excitedly. "Come along, there's a good boy, I've got someone over here dying to meet you——" She seized his hand and dragged him, half laughing, half protesting, into the heart of the crowd, leaving Rosamund to assimilate this new bit of information.

So this was Basil, Eileen's one-time husband: the young man who, according to Lindy's account, had left Eileen because she was always in a fluster of overwork, always making him feel guilty. Did this interpretation dovetail in any degree with the opinions that Basil himself had just been expressing to Rosamund about marriage—presumably based on his own experience? In all this noise and confusion it was difficult to think coherently, or at any length, but so far as she could collate her memories, it did not seem that there was much connection between the two versions— though she supposed they weren't actually incompatible. You could, of course, object to the state of marriage as such *and* find your wife irritating. . . . Realising that by standing here speculating she was in danger of looking neglected—an unforgiveable sin at a party— Rosamund decided to worm her way through the crowd until she caught sight of someone she knew. The room, which at first had seemed full of neighbours, now seemed full of total strangers, more and more pouring in every moment, like refugees from some unimaginable disaster outside: the lucky ones, the survivors, gathering themselves into the shelter of Lindy's charm. . . .

And now here was Lindy herself again, only a yard or two away. Over the intervening shoulders, Rosamund was able to witness the introduction of Basil to this person who was "dying to meet him". It was Eileen. Rosamund could not hear what was being said; she could see only the expression of baffled dismay on Eileen's face, of utter astonishment on Basil's. And the smile, the warm, charming hostess smile on Lindy's, and her mouth opening and shutting, pouring forth animated, inaudible words.

What was she saying? Why was Eileen looking so appalled? And Basil so surprised? Had he not known that Eileen would be here? Did he perhaps not even know that Eileen lived here at all? Was Lindy trying to "bring them together" by the childish ruse of a surprise meeting? No. Lindy would never be so silly—nor so simple. Whatever she was up to, it would be something complicated, and carefully planned. It would be like a card trick—all those simple, natural smiles and gestures would culminate—surprise! surprise!—in Lindy's suddenly appearing to advantage in relation to something else—presumably, in this case, Eileen.

But there was no chance of filling in the details from this distance, so Rosamund continued on her difficult way until she reached the French windows, which had been flung open to the September night, still almost as warm as summer. The lantern so carefully wired up by Geoffrey hung from the laburnum tree, and on the shadowy space of grass sat or stood little clusters of guests, in comparative quietness and freedom of movement.

Among the groups Rosamund caught sight of the Dawsons, Mrs Dawson's plump bare arms and careless frizz of grey-blonde hair shining palely through the darkness; and she could hear Mr Dawson's elderly yet boyish voice holding forth about sparrow-hawks. Rosamund could not quite see whom he was addressing, but at least he and his wife were well-known to her, so she unobtrusively sidled into the group, exchanging with Mrs. Dawson the conspiratorial smiles of women tolerating good-naturedly the incomprehensible male passion for talking about facts,

when there is so much else in the world so immeasurably
more interesting.

"And I *know* it wasn't a pigeon!" Mr Dawson was
asserting forcefully, defending the opinion against some
imaginary opponent. It must be imaginary, for surely he
couldn't have magnified into an opponent either his wife
or the blonde, beautifully lacquered lady who was regard-
ing him amiably but with a certain restlessness across her
gin and lemon. "Sparrow-hawks don't necessarily hover,
you know. Everybody thinks they do, but they don't. They
dart under the trees. It's ridiculous to say that just because
it wasn't hovering it must have been a pigeon!"

The lacquered lady hadn't said so, and was beginning to
look a little resentful as well as restless. But she was wrong
to take it personally: she should have realised that she
was only the stand-in for a dream-audience of attentive,
admiring professional naturalists. "*Some* people think
you don't ever see them in towns—" he was moving triumphantly to his peroration—"but that's quite untrue. And
anyway, you can't call this exactly 'town', can you?
. . . All those great elms. . . ." He gestured vaguely, and
stared out across the rooftops with the wistful intensity
of imagination cultivated by so many suburbanites—they
can at will raze to the ground acres of red brick and
wooden fencing, and see in primeval splendour the rural
remnants of their environment. "It's practically woodland,
you know, over there behind the tennis-club buildings.
You could easily have a pair nesting there. Several
pairs."

"Yes, I'm sure you could," said the blonde lady,
rather helplessly. Rosamund could see that she was trying to make up for the blankness of her mind on the
subject by a sudden look of bright attentiveness, and by
sipping her drink continuously. Rosamund felt sorry for Mr
Dawson, and tried to think of something encouraging to
say about sparrow-hawks herself. It was nice to know
they were there, and she wished them well, but that
seemed rather a feeble thing to say.

But Mr Dawson mercifully did not seem sensitive to
the inadequacy of his audience. He was happily continuing: "But of course, people don't *look*. They never see
anything of the wild life here because they never look
for it. They think that because they live in a street of

houses and people, nothing else can exist there. Did you realise—" he turned once more in fruitless challenge to the blonde lady—"that there are more worms in London than there are people? Did you know that?"

How had he found out? Or, rather, how had the writer of whatever article he had been reading found out? Did the L.C.C. pay somebody to count worms? Or did universities provide grants for it? What odd ways there were of spending your life, if you were so minded. But poor Mr Dawson was evidently waiting for a proper response to his dramatic announcement. "Really? You don't say" wasn't enough.

"Well, I think that's perfectly splendid!" contributed Rosamund. "I mean, when you look at all the crowds of people in Oxford Street, and read about the population explosion and everything, there's something awfully consoling in thinking that worms are doing it too. You feel it's all part of Nature after all."

Mr Dawson seemed a little non-plussed. Evidently, in spite of her good intentions, she had failed to strike quite the right note. At this point, Mrs Dawson intervened, in her comfortable voice: "Harold's always been interested in the Country," she observed, as if in vague excuse for the whole conversation, including Rosamund's contribution. "When he was younger, he used to toy with the idea of living there, didn't you, dear?"

"Toy with it! It was always my ambition. Always. You know that. I wanted to be a farmer. But Life brought me other duties: I've had to face the fact that the buttercup fields are not for me." He sighed.

"If you'd really been a farmer, you'd have learnt to hate buttercups long ago," remarked his wife comfortably. "Farmers always do." She seemed not at all put out by his little speech, though the "other duties" which had frustrated his ambition could be none other than herself and the two sons with which she had presented him. "It's beginning to be a little chilly, dear, don't you think?" she continued, shrugging up her bare shoulders expressively. "Don't you think we should be getting indoors?"

"Of course, dear!" At once Mr Dawson was all solicitude, helping his wife from her chair, escorting her across the grass towards the bright indoors: and it was only then that Rosamund noticed that Lindy, from just by the open French window, seemed to be watching them. She might, of course, have just been looking out, with hospitable concern, to make sure that her guests in the garden were all enjoying themselves, and were well supplied with food and drink. But Rosamund chose to interpret it otherwise. There she is again, she told herself, watching like Big Brother to see if she can't catch some wife nagging her husband, or being possessive about him, or something like that. She probably thinks that Mrs Dawson isn't feeling cold at all, but is dragging her husband indoors to get him away from that dull blonde who can't even talk intelligently about sparrow-hawks! She's going to come over and tell us so tomorrow morning, I know she is: and I shall have to feed her coffee and biscuits while she goes on and on about it. And then she's going to say how awful it is of her to have prevented him becoming a farmer: and when I say that he's only too thankful to have been prevented, he much prefers a comfortable life really, then Lindy will say . . . she'll say . . .

Rosamund could not think of the smiling, subtly deflating remark with which Lindy would silence her in this imaginary conversation. Indeed, by this time Rosamund was quite losing sight of the fact that the foregoing conversation *was* imaginary. And she certainly wasn't allowing herself to reflect that it was most unlikely that Lindy could have heard anything at all that the Dawsons were saying to each other out on the lawn.

For since the drive to Mother's this afternoon, Lindy had swollen in Rosamund's imagination into a figure of superhuman power and cunning: nothing, nobody, could escape her net. Why, even now she must be noticing, storing up, the fact that Rosamund and Geoffrey had not spoken to each other at all since arriving at the party. And yet, if Rosamund sought him out and spoke to him, then that, too, would be noted: as possessiveness. And if Rosamund were to leave the party early, as she now longed to do, that would count as a gesture of jealous resentment; if, on the other hand, she stayed to the bitter end, then it would be to keep watch on her husband . . . to make sure he wasn't enjoying the company of other women too much. . . .

Suddenly, her conversation earlier in the evening with

Eileen's husband swept back into Rosamund's memory with a new significance. When Basil complained about people continually watching his marriage for symptoms of breakdown, had "people" been a euphemism for "Lindy"? Or had his sister-in-law's evil watchfulness so poisoned his whole environment that he really did feel that "everybody" was doing it? Rosamund could picture Lindy sitting attentive in the newly-weds' little flat, noticing whether Basil kissed his wife the moment he came in at the front door, or whether he looked at his letters on the hall table first. . . . Whether Eileen ran out of the kitchen to greet him. . . .

She's a sort of vampire! thought Rosamund in sudden, uncontrollable loathing. She lives on the flaws in other people's marriages . . . she sucks the blood from them, leaving a dried-up, bloodless ruin where once was a relationship. . . . And then doesn't even want the husband for herself!

Or does she? Does she? Does she want Basil . . . ? Does she want Geoffrey . . . ?

Rosumund's one idea now was to get away from this horrible party unnoticed. She pushed her way blindly through the sitting room, through the hall; and as she passed the foot of the stairs she felt quite sure that she could hear Eileen upstairs, crying.

But it was absurd, really. She couldn't have. Even if Eileen *was* crying, she couldn't possibly have heard it, there was far too much noise everywhere. Nevertheless, she carried the imagined sound out of the house with her, like an armful of extra fuel, all ready to fling upon the flames of her hatred once she was blessedly alone, within her own four quiet walls.

CHAPTER X

That first expedition in Lindy's car proved, as Rosamund had feared, to be the prelude to an entirely new pattern for their weekends. At first Lindy backed up her con-

tinued insistence on driving them to Geoffrey's mother's
by alleging various reasons of her own for wanting to go
to that particular neighbourhood on that particular Sunday: but gradually this pretence—if pretence it was—
was abandoned, and it became simply the accepted thing
that she should take them. Soon it also became the accepted thing that she should spend the whole afternoon there with them; for Mrs Fielding had taken a great
fancy to Lindy and was always urging her to stay.

And so it came about that every fortnight or so the
three of them would go off together in the car, spend
the afternoon together with Mrs Fielding, and come back
together in the evening, for all the world as if Lindy were
one of the family, a daughter, or a sister, or something.
Or Geoffrey's wife, of course.

As the autumn advanced, slow and golden, with its
bright shortening days, the habit of going out with Lindy
began to spread to the intervening Sundays as well—
the Sundays they had been accustomed to spend getting
up late, pottering about the house, and reading out to each
other astonishing or ridiculous items from the vast un-
manageable Sunday papers which gradually spread so cosily all over everything as the leisurely day wore on.
But not any more. Rosamund was learning to dread this
endless, cloudless St Martin's summer, or whatever it
was called: this waking, Sunday after Sunday, to the
still, misty mornings, with a golden promise behind the
mist that grew and grew until about ten o'clock it burst
into the full glory of the sun.

And always with the sun came Lindy, her head sticking over the wall—or through the kitchen window—or
round the front door—and her gay voice calling: "Isn't it a
gorgeous day? Shall we go out somewhere?" And after a
while, it ceased to be "Shall we go out?" and became
"Where shall we go?" so fixed and regular had these
Sunday expeditions become. And then there was the
little excited huddle over the map . . . where to go . . .
how long it would take . . . whether to take a picnic lunch
or stop at a pub. . . . Rosamund forced herself to join in
these debates good-humouredly—indeed, the other two
always consulted her opinions most punctiliously—but she
never managed to make any suggestions half as enterprising and imaginative as Lindy's. Her imagination

was elsewhere, far from the sunny promise of the morning; in dark, cloud-hung, shadowy places, where it rained, and rained, and rained.

But it never did rain, not all that autumn long, or so it seemed to Rosamund. Week after week they drove along narrow sunlit lanes; they picnicked among warm tussocks of dry autumn grass; they picked late blackberries in the mellow afternoons; and never did the rain come.

Eileen never came with them. Lindy had brushed this idea aside, right at the beginning, with the casual verdict: "She doesn't care for this sort of thing." Shang Low came, however, although he didn't seem to care for this sort of thing either. He was always put on the back seat with Rosamund and urged to be a good dog, which, according to the letter of the law, she supposed he was. That is to say, he no longer ventured to snarl at her, or set up his former ferocious yapping at the sight of her. Instead, he sat as far away as he could on the warm leather seat and watched her, his eyes bulging with dislike and suspicion. Her occasional reluctant advances of friendship he met by withdrawing his dignified little body even further into its chosen niche, and very slightly increasing the tempo of his stertorous breathing. Not a threat, exactly; just an indication. If, rashly, she went further, and offered him some titbit of cold chicken or beef from the picnic, he would take it into his mouth, hold it there motionless for about thirty seconds, and then, slowly and deliberately, watching her face all the time, would spit it carefully out onto the seat of the car.

So Rosamund soon gave up all attempt to get on terms with him on these expeditions, and they sat silently, as far away from each other as the seat allowed, in a state of mutual dislike so intense that it almost became a sort of bond between them. Companions in enmity, they listened to the chatter and laughter on the front seat, occasionally exchanging a suspicious, hostile glance when one or the other of them, in their restless boredom, made some unwonted movement.

But Shang Low was charming with Geoffrey. As soon as they settled down on the grass for the picnic, he would come bundling out of the car and hurry to Geoffrey's side. He would put his front paws on Geoffrey's knee and stare unblinkingly and with adoring greed at his adopted master's every mouthful. From Geoffrey's hand he would even eat plain bread with mustard on it. Lindy and Geoffrey would laugh at him when he did this; tease each other about Shang Low's growing devotion, and play idiotic games with him. They would kneel on the grass a few feet apart, with Shang Low in the middle, and both call him at once and see whom he went to first: and whichever it was, it seemed to be equally uproariously funny, Rosamund noted sourly. Sometimes she tried to join in, exploiting humourously her role as Shang Low's enemy, only to find that she wasn't being humourous at all, just rather dull and interrupting.

Not that either of them said, or even hinted this. They were both very kind, and did their best to treat her as one of them. But Rosamund knew for herself that all the spark, the wit, had gone out of her. The thing that used to flash unbidden and scarcely noticed between her and Geoffrey was gone. Rosamund was learning the first sharp lesson that hits the tolerant, broad-minded wife; the wife who determines to avoid nagging and scenes, and determines to win her husband back simply by being as good humoured and nice to him as ever. She learns that being good humoured and nice isn't a one-way process, and never was; it is a response to something and when that something isn't there, then the good humour and niceness begin to look peculiar, almost crazy, like playing tennis with no one on the other side of the net; it just makes people stare. So you just have to stop playing, and stand dull and incapable, while on the next court the Other Woman returns all the balls—or even misses them; at least she is playing. And your man may well be thinking: Why, my wife used to play like this once: why is she no good at it any more, just standing there like that, so stiff and dull?

Was Geoffrey noticing that she had grown stiff and dull? Sometimes she fancied that he was looking at her, a little puzzled. Was he wondering what was the matter with her, why she had ceased to be an amusing companion? Or was he even beginning to believe that she had always been like this—that his memories of her as a lively, entertaining personality were an illusion?

Lindy has destroyed us, Rosamund reflected, with a

sort of dispassionate wonder, one cloudless October afternoon. Without seducing him, without so much as exchanging a kiss, she has succeeded in laying my marriage in ruins. *She* knows it already, of course; but does Geoffrey?

Through eyes half closed against the low sun, she examined her husband's face, bronzed, sunburnt, content. Probably he was only aware, so far, that time passed somehow much more pleasantly and amusingly when Lindy was there than when she wasn't; he might even suppose that Rosamund found this too—she had been at enough pains, after all, to pretend that this was the case. He looked so happy as he sat there, in the mellow autumn light, so unsuspecting. He didn't know yet that they were walking in a ruined city with all its lovely buildings fallen, with gaping chasms in the once solid streets. She almost found herself crying out to him aloud: Look out...! Look out...!

And then the going home—not to their own home, oh no: it had become established custom that after these expeditions they should go back to Lindy's for a drink before dinner; to sit in her delightful sitting room (which so maddeningly just caught the last of the evening sun, and so looked at its very best at just this time) and talk about the pleasures of the day. Rosamund always joined in the conversation adequately enough, but all the time her mind was inclined to wander round this charming room hoping to find some dreadful flaw; some hideous streak of vulgarity or tastelessness. But it was no good. Sometimes the room was untidy, but always charmingly so: a swathe of Lindy's newly designed material flung across a chair, a pile of coloured wools awaiting sorting, a tangle of indoor plants gathered onto a tray for watering. Everywhere there seemed to be pictures, brilliant fabrics, flowers. Shamelessly, Rosamund looked at each bit of furniture in turn, picturing it, with nostalgic yearning, as it had appeared on the afternoon of the move; drab, shabby, and uninviting. Why couldn't it look like that again? And why couldn't Lindy look again like that dumpy, uninteresting little woman they has seen leaning into the van? Rosamund dreamed of that long-ago afternoon as a traveller in the desert dreams of clear water.

And so the autumn wore on, turned at last to winter. With the darkness, and the coming of the fogs, the char-

acter of their Sunday expeditions changed, but they
did not cease. They went to museums now, and to art
galleries, and to look at old buildings; and it slowly
dawned on Rosamund that this way of life had come to
stay.

It was on an evening in early December when this
thought finally crystallised in her mind; an evening of thin,
chilling fog creeping up from the pavements, drifting
down from the low blanket of a starless London sky. The
sort of evening to send workers and wayfarers hurrying
home, head down, their minds full of some bright cosy
room full of warmth and welcome. A room like Lindy's.
Why should any man ever tire of the thought that a room
like this was waiting for him? Why should so innocent, and
yet so rewarding, a relationship ever come to an end?
Rosamund realised that all this time she had been waiting, at the back of her mind, for things to come to a head;
for some sort of a showdown. She saw now, quite clearly,
that there would quite likely never be one; she would have
to endure this threesome for always.

It was strange that it should have been on this evening,
of all evenings, that Rosamund should have come to this
fatalistic conclusion. For already, although she could not
know it, the showdown was at hand.

CHAPTER XI

When Rosamund woke the next morning, she did not yet
realise that she had caught 'flu; it would be another
twenty-four hours before the symptoms became unmis-
takeable. She knew that she had passed a restless, half
wakeful night, and that she now felt depressed and tired,
disturbed by a vague sense of foreboding: but her anxiety
and unhappiness about her husband and Lindy seemed
quite enough to account for all this. She lay for a few minutes after the alarm had gone, weighed down by a dreadful reluctance to do anything at all. Getting up, cooking
breakfast, tidying the house, all seemed equally impos-

sible. And when she remembered that this was the day for the coffee morning at Norah's, her depression unexpectedly deepened. For usually she greatly enjoyed these sessions of gossip and problem-airing, in spite of the fact that they had been Lindy's idea in the first place. Within a few days of moving into the neighbourhood, Lindy had expressed herself astonished that no such activity existed among the local housewives. But *everybody* has been having them for *years,* she had declared wonderingly: they were such *fun,* and such a good way of getting to know the neighbours . . . of giving the housebound young mothers the chance of a little intelligent conversation.

She turned out to be perfectly right, of course: the meetings *were* fun, and achieved everything she had predicted of them. The shy and the housebound, as well as the notably un-shy and the opinionated, came flocking to the first meeting, held in Lindy's charming sitting room. Lindy had started things off with an amusing little speech about her trip to America three years ago, and of course that had led to a lovely discussion about the evils of affluence— always a delightful topic to discuss in affluent surroundings. It had been agreed that they should meet once a fortnight, in each others' houses, each in turn acting as hostess. It was a splendid idea, the only snag being that Lindy had started off the cycle with such a lavish supply of refreshments that the succeeding hostesses were left with a major problem on their hands: whether to keep up with her over-generous standards, or to risk appearing mean. Rosamund, summoning all her courage, had tried to reverse the trend when it came to her turn, and had firmly produced nothing but biscuits to accompany the coffee: and the look of relief on all the faces at the sight of this modest display had led her (rashly) to suppose that the entertainment would from now on establish itself at this manageable level.

But almost at once the standards began creeping up again. The next hostess after Rosamund produced biscuits and a plate of little scones, which she declared, a little apologetically, she "happened to have just made". The next one produced, without apology, biscuits, scones, and a huge chocolate cake: the next one biscuits, buttered buns, cheese tartlets, and meringues. By now it was a landslide. Sandwiches, smörgasbord, olives, sausages on sticks, half a dozen different kinds of cake—these were what poor Norah had to contend with. It was no wonder that when she rang Rosamund, in desperation, just after breakfast, she spoke of these fast-multiplying delicacies as if they were advancing enemy troops, and her home the beleaguered citadel.

". . . and I thought, with the fruit cake, that would be enough," she was gabbling. "Because of course I was going to do the drop-scones last thing before we started, so they'd be hot. But I've only just got the sausage rolls in the oven now, there'll never be time for the macaroons as well, they have to have such a cool oven. I shan't even be able to *start* them before ten! Oh, Rosamund, *what* do you think everyone would think if I simply ran out and *bought* a cake?"

She paused on this appalling suggestion for long enough to let it sink in, but not long enough for Rosamund to reply. "It seems so awful," she continued unhappily. "After that time at Rhoda's! *Five* different kinds of cake—do you remember?—all home made! And those shrimp things in aspic; and . . ."

"Why not let Rhoda win?" suggested Rosamund bracingly. "*Someone's* got to, in the end. Just give us biscuits, Norah. No one *wants* all that food in the middle of the morning. It's ridiculous!"

"I know, I know!" wailed Norah. "But what can you do? Oh. . . . They're burning . . . !"

The receiver at the other end crashed down. Rosamund, feeling quite revived now by the thought of the five different kinds of cake that she wasn't having to make, set about her work quite energetically, and was ready to start for Norah's in plenty of time not to be offered a lift in Lindy's car. There was something peculiarly dreadful about Lindy's small acts of kindness towards her. It wasn't so bad when Geoffrey was there too— you could then feel that she was acting a part for his benefit; but when he wasn't, you didn't know what to feel. All these little obliging actions, interspersed with subtly spiteful remarks—what did they really mean? A more charitable character than Rosamund would no doubt suggest that Lindy's bark was worse than her bite; but what consolation in this when it is always the bark that is ringing in your ears?

In spite of Rosamund's early start, Lindy was there first. She was already comfortably settled in one of the cretonne-covered armchairs in Norah's sitting room, and Rosamund could see at once that she was being charming. No one would have guessed from her flattering comments on Norah's pictures, her wall-paper, her iced walnut cake and the view from her window that the speaker considered Norah to be a nagging wife, a possessive and incompetent mother. Though of course, Rosamund reminded herself, there was no real inconsistency, lots of nagging wives live in pretty houses. . . .

"Whatever are you looking at me like that for?"

Lindy finished on a slight laugh, as if the question was being asked jokingly. But Rosamund had a queer feeling that it hadn't started like that at all; it was as if the words had been startled from Lindy by some sudden shock, from which, with swift effort, she had recovered herself. But what sort of a shock? And what *had* Rosamund been looking like? A quick glance into the mirror above Norah's mantelpiece of course only revealed what mirrors always do reveal—the controlled, appraising look of one who wants to see what she looks like.

So Rosamund laughed too.

"I was just surprised that you've beaten me to it," she explained. "I didn't notice you passing me in the road—or didn't you come in the car?"

"Yes. Yes, I came in the car." Lindy still seemed to be watching her intently. Then: "Did you see Basil last night?" she asked sharply, as Norah left the room for a minute.

Rosamund was taken aback at the unexpected question. She hadn't seen Basil for weeks—had almost forgotten his existence.

"No. Why? Did he say he was coming?"

"No. I just wondered." Lindy did not seem to understand that further elucidation was called for. "He didn't telephone, or anything?" she persisted.

"No. Why should he? We hardly know him. I only ever met him that once, you know, that time at your party. . . ."

"But you seemed to get to know him quite well then. I saw you talking together for ages. What did you think of him? Do tell me."

Lindy was leaning forward now, intent and anxious,

and Rosamund had an odd sense of a sudden small shifting of power between them—an indefinable change in the balance of their relationship. For a moment it made her physically dizzy, like an earth tremor beneath them both. The room seemed to quiver, she felt sick and shivering, but of course this could have been the beginning of her 'flu: anyway, it passed quickly, and she found herself answering:

"Well, it's quite a while ago now, you know, but I remember thinking he was quite amusing. Yes, I liked him, really. He seems a rather impulsive young man, though. . . ."

She was being guarded. She had the uneasy feeling that whatever she said on this topic was going to be used against her in some way—or rather, against Eileen, though by what devious means this could come about she could not imagine. But nothing more could be said now, for here was Norah back with another plate of food— plainly, she had ignored every scrap of Rosamund's advice on the telephone—and behind her came three or four new arrivals; and the consequent confusions of greetings, exclamations and enquiries made further private conversation impossible.

The next half hour was devoted to the passing round of food and cups. About half the company fell to with gusto, forgetful both of their figures and of the future terrors of competitive hostess-craft; the other half vied with one another in that highly complex art of registering the utmost delight and enthusiasm about all kinds of cakes and pastries without actually eating any of them.

This ritual over, Norah's worried little face relaxed a little as she surveyed the victorious mounds of left-overs which, like the survivors of a well-deployed army, had brought glory to their general: and now the discussion began.

As usual, it started with somebody's travels to somewhere, but within minutes everyone, speaker included, was talking about their children, competing, like Hyde Park orators, for an audience for their particular problem.

The mothers of the teenagers won, of course: the owners of babies or toddlers didn't stand a chance in the competition. For how pale and shadowy has toilet-train-ing become during the last few years; and demand-feeding; and jealousy of the new baby; all the issues which not so long ago used to rock society from the top-most teaching hospitals to the humblest young mother at her welfare clinic, filling the newspapers and magazines with their backwash as they passed. These once momentous questions have now been thrust back into the narrow nursery world from which they so mysteriously arose. Use your common sense, the young mothers are told nowadays: their brief glory is over.

Not so the mothers of the teenagers. Nothing so dull as common sense is demanded of *them*. The notoriety of their children's age group inevitably rubs off a little on to them, and hitherto unremarkable housewives suddenly find themselves in the position of V.I.P.'s, albeit of a secondary and reflected kind.

And so it came about that Rosamund, Norah, and a brisk, very young-looking brunette called Carlotta stepped undisputed into the limelight of this little company, simply by virtue of owning one or two each of these extraordinary creatures about whom so many millions of words are day after day poured forth. It had been like this for two or three years already for Rosamund, but she still enjoyed it. "We've *got* one!" she could say of Peter, as if he were a Great Auk's egg, or a burglar alarm that unfolded into a coffee table; and the uninitiated would at once turn to her, attentive, respectful, and full of solemn questions. And it hardly mattered how she answered; everything she said was listened to with awe and wonderment, as were the travellers' tales of long ago: she might have been an explorer, newly returned from some dangerous and uncharted jungle. What is it *like*, people would say, wide-eyed; what *happens*?

But this morning her unearned notoriety was less enjoyable than usual, for of late, for the first time, she had begun to think of Peter as a problem instead of merely as a nuisance. Not that Peter had changed particularly. He was really no lazier, no more unpredictable, no worse mannered than he had been for ages; it was just that he and his failings seemed to matter more. As the happiness of Rosamund's marriage slowly drained away it was leaving Peter and his sins sticking up like a jagged rock, right in the middle of everything; you could no longer float past and over them on smooth sunlit waters. She felt sure that Geoffrey was aware of the change, too: his relationship with his son was deteriorating as she watched. Not that he called Peter to order more than he had before, or was more severe; if anything he was less so. But his reprimands, when they came, were unhappy and irritable where once they had been confident; as if, Rosamund fancied, he resented having to be bothered with the boy's misdemeanours—resented, perhaps, having to be bothered with his home life at all. Or as if his eyes had been opened to imperfections in a way they had never been in the old happy days. A skilful teacher he had at his command, one who could train and develop sensitivity to domestic imperfections as if it were a precious artistic gift.

So Rosamund's contributions to the debate this morning were a little sombre; so too were Norah's. Norah, very tentatively, allowed herself to enjoy for just a little while her prestige as the owner of the most nearly delinquent son of their little circle, but never for long. Ned's misdoings always earned her a good deal of interest and sympathy, and would have earned more but for her habit of whitewashing, as well as worrying about, everything he did. The resultant bewildering tangle of worry and whitewash threw everyone into some uncertainty, no one feeling sure where sympathy would be appropriate and where it would merely throw her into a nervous fluster of retractions and explanations.

Carlotta's recital came next. No problems here, but the same unbroken success story as had been deflating all her friends for years, ever since the days of her unnaturally natural pregnancies when she had felt so much less sick than anyone else and had produced bigger babies with shorter labours and fewer stitches than anyone could imagine. The way she'd talked about it, you'd think that the babies were mere by-products of the process; no more than incidental trophies designed to commemorate Carlotta's capacity for Radiant Motherhood. You kept waiting for something to go wrong, but nothing ever did: and now here was the first of these products getting nine O-levels and a prize for physics—a tribute this time to his mother's qualities as a Whole Woman.

"Of course," Carlotta explained. "I'm particularly

pleased that he's not done too badly" (Oh, the dreadful mock-modesty of the mothers of successful sons!) "because everyone has always told me that they were bound to suffer from my going out to work. They'd grow up deprived, people said: delinquent; and that I'd wear myself out, doing two jobs all the time. But they don't seem to be turning out so badly; and I don't think that I seem so *terribly* worn out, do I, compared with other women of my age?"

She must know very well that she looked at least ten years younger than any of them, far too young to be the mother of a sixth-former; but nevertheless everyone played up and assured her all over again that she *did* look as young as all this. You had to play the game according to the rules, no matter what flamboyant cards people laid down, or else what about when it came to *your* turn?

Rosamund glanced over at Lindy, who had not spoken all this time. Was she, for once, feeling left out? After all, she was the only one of them who had come unequipped with any problem whatsoever—not even an outdated one like a toddler not eating spinach, which used to be such a winner years ago.

But Lindy was looking as contented, as pleased with herself as ever: not in the least bored or at a loss. On the contrary, she wore a rather tiresome air of being the outsider who sees most of the game, thus turning her initial disadvantage into a potentially winning card.

But she didn't even bother to use it. Even as Rosamund watched, she bent down and began to collect her bag and gloves together.

"I'm awfully afraid I've got to go now," she said to Norah, standing up. "Don't let me break up the party, though: I'll just slip out."

Norah broke into little anxious protests, getting to her feet at the same time. Must Lindy really go? It was barely half past twelve . . . ?

"Yes, Lindy, do stay," urged Carlotta. "After all, *you* can arrange your work when you like! You don't have to clock-in like us poor wage-slaves!"

"No, I know," said Lindy smiling. "It's not *work*, exactly, that I have to go for. It's some typing I've promised to do for an old lady in the country. Such a dear old thing, and so full of go! Well over seventy, and she's

started writing a book on archaeology—proving that Evans
was absolutely right about Knossos—if all this means anything to you——" she amended apologetically to the company at large. "*I* didn't know anything about it either until
I got to know her; but she makes it so terribly interesting. . . . Anyway, I *must* go now, because I said I'd have
this instalment all ready to take down to her this afternoon . . . so cheerio, everybody . . ." Smiling, calling
friendly goodbyes, she disappeared into the hall with
Norah; and a minute later the front door closed.

Rosamund felt her limbs shaking. Heat and cold
chased each other, like laughing children, up and down
her spine. She could feel her face going white.

So Lindy, not herself, was to help her mother-in-law
with the new book! Rosamund had never even been told
that there was to *be* a book. After all her years of helping, sympathising, sharing in the old lady's hobby, this
fascinating project had been kept a secret from her! Or—
perhaps even worse—perhaps Mrs Fielding just hadn't
bothered to tell her—had been so absorbed in discussing
it with her new helper that she hadn't thought about
Rosamund at all. Admittedly, Rosamund had missed the
last Sunday visit—Geoffrey and Lindy had gone on their
own, for almost the only time—but even so, there were letters, weren't there? Telephones? And anyway, a project
like this doesn't leap into life in five minutes—Mrs Fielding must have been thinking about it for weeks.

Somehow this lesser blow seemed to strike with a
violence that Rosamund had never yet experienced, in
all these months. Perhaps because it was so utterly
unexpected—a blow from the side instead of the front,
so that all her guards were down. Whatever the reason, she
experienced now waves of such bare, uncontrollable
jealousy that she felt she was going to faint. Her mother-
in-law—Jessie——the old, welcoming house—they were all
Lindy's now. She wasn't content with just Geoffrey.

And when she got home she found on the hall table a
note from Geoffrey—he must have dashed in at lunch time,
found her out, and left it there:

> "Late back tonight. Don't wait supper
>   Love—Geoff"

Not "Geoffrey" any more, but "Geoff".
Everything was Lindy's now.

CHAPTER XII

"Lindy's disappeared!"

Sitting giddily on the edge of the bed, just outside the circle of lamplight, Rosamund stared into her husband's face almost uncomprehending. For one mad second it seemed the most natural thing in the world that Lindy should have disappeared, for in her dream Rosamund had killed her. How could she be expected to reappear after that?

"Don't look so blank, darling!" Geoffrey urged her impatiently (over the last weeks, "darling" had imperceptibly changed from an endearment to an expression of dutifully repressed irritation). "Just tell me—do you know where she is?"

Rosamund felt the unstable heat of fever leaping in her face: inside her skull was an aching and a roaring which made it difficult to make sense of Geoffrey's words, simple though they were and desperately though she tried to do so as she felt his irritation and anxiety mounting. Strange that her muddled brain should be aware so clearly of his feelings, and yet be so confused about his words.

"No—I haven't seen her," she blurted out at last, and felt her ears ring with weariness at the mental effort involved.

But it only let her in for more questions.

"Not at all? Not all day? Didn't she say anything to you about where she was going? Or ring up, or something?"

Rosamund was puzzled, not so much by his disproportionate anxiety as by the odd fact that it somehow didn't strike her as disproportionate. Surely it should have? Lindy was a grown woman; why shouldn't she be out and about past nine in the evening without giving an account of herself?

But her head was clearing now. She was becoming capable of examining the question rationally, of seeing how unreasonable was her husband's perturbation.

"No, she didn't. Should she have? Surely she's just out seeing friends, or something?"

"But she said—she told me. . . . Oh, I don't know. Perhaps you're right. . . . Perhaps I'm making too much of it—" she could see that Geoffrey was trying to pull himself together—"but it was such a shock, somehow, finding the house all dark . . . no heating on . . . the little dog yapping. . . . I've never seen it like that before."

Geoffrey was quite shaken, she could see, and she could a little bit understand his feelings, irrational though of course they were. She, too, albeit unwillingly, associated Lindy's house with warmth, bright lights, comfort. Even to her, who disliked and feared Lindy, it would have been a little bit of a shock to find the house as Geoffrey described it; how much more so for him! She tried to be consoling as well as reasonable.

"Well, I'm sure there's nothing to worry about. She's sure to be back soon. And what about Eileen?" she added, wondering why she hadn't thought of this before. "Won't she know something?"

"She can't. She's not there—she's been staying with that girl since the weekend—Wait a minute, though—I wonder? . . . I might ring her . . . see if she's had some message. . . ."

He ran down the stairs again, leaving the bedroom door wide open, and soon Rosamund heard his voice in the hall:

"Hullo? Yes. Yes, that's right, Eileen Forbes. Yes, if you would: thanks." A long pause, and then: "Oh, Eileen, I'm glad I've caught you. I was wondering if you knew where Lindy is? She was going to call for me at the office" (this was the first Rosamund had heard of it, but it seemed of no importance now) "but she never turned up. And she's not at home either . . . it's dark and shut up . . . what? No, I don't know. She just said there was something she wanted to tell me about. But she hasn't even taken the car, it's still outside the house. . . . Yes, I thought of that; but it's not as foggy as all that; it seems to be clearing. Anyway, she could have rung me, or come by tube or something. It's not like her."

Here there was a long pause, during which Geoffrey said "Yes" more times than Rosamund could count, each time, it seemed, sounding more anxious and mystified. At last he began to speak intelligibly again.

"Yes. Yes, I know. That's what's worrying me, too.

She'd never have left him shut up like that in the cold and dark all this time. He was yapping his head off when I went in."

More silence at this end; then Geoffrey's voice again: "Well, I know, Eileen, I wish it as much as you do; but I *didn't* ask her, and there it is. Besides, she mightn't have been able to tell me over the phone; it must have been something fairly confidential, for her to want to meet me specially away from home. And urgent, too. She sounded as if she was somehow scared. . . . That's why I'm so worried. . . ."

A few more brief, inconclusive sentences, and then Rosamund heard the telephone ring off. Geoffrey came slowly up the stairs.

"I expect you heard all that," he said briefly. "It hasn't made us much the wiser, has it?"

Rosamund was touched by the "us". Did he really suppose that she was worrying about Lindy, too?

"I heard your end of it," she pointed out. "But not Eileen's. Hasn't she any ideas?"

"Not really. She thinks it's odd, though, just as I do: not *like* Lindy. But Eileen'll be home tonight, she says— she was just setting out when I rang. She'll be here in an hour or two. Perhaps she'll have thought of something . . . or perhaps Lindy will be home by then. . . ."

His voice softened, lightened, at this possibility. Rosamund felt strangely moved by his emotion, abhorrent though its cause was to her. Trying to ignore the dizziness, the fierce headache that assailed her whenever she moved, she stood up, hoping Geoffrey would not notice that she had been lying down. To impose her own illness on him just when he was worrying about Lindy would be terrible, just the sort of thing that neurotic neglected wives are always doing.

"Let's go over to Lindy's and look around, right now," she suggested, fighting back the throbbing inside her skull, the blackness that was threatening to blot out the room as she stood upright. For a moment it seemed that she must fall . . . but just in time the light returned. . . . Geoffrey's face swung back into her view. With one foot, she began feeling surreptitiously for her shoes beside the bed, ready to implement her suggestion. "She might have left a note there for Eileen, or something," she hazarded.

"I've looked. There's nothing," said Geoffrey flatly: and then "Well, I don't know, I was only looking round quickly, of course. I might have missed something. *You* go, Rosamund, would you? You'll have more idea what to look for. I don't want both of us to be gone at once, she might ring up here."

Again Rosamund was touched, in spite of herself, by the way Geoffrey was treating her as a partner in anxiety; and a respected partner, too, to judge by that "You'll have more idea what to look for." It made her feel stronger, less dizzy, the sort of person who could easily walk across a room and down some stairs. Her questing toes encountered the shoes at last, and she slipped her feet into them unobtrusively, without looking down, for fear of drawing Geoffrey's attention to her actions. Not that there seemed to be much risk of this; he was still frowning, deeply pre-occupied.

"How do I get in—have you the key?" she asked, ready, now, for the little expedition. "Or did you leave the door unlocked?"

"*She* left the door unlocked," said Geoffrey, the anxiety wiped momentarily from his face by a look of amused, reminiscent affection. "You know what she is—so trusting and happy-go-lucky!"

He talks as if she's still alive! flashed through Rosamund's mind for one absurd, inexplicable moment. Then reason and common sense returned, and she thrust away the fantastic implications of the thought. She prepared, instead, to control the familiar surge of anger she was bound to feel at that "trusting and happy-go-lucky".

But it didn't come. Was she too weak with fever to be capable of any strong emotion? But it didn't feel like weakness at all—quite the reverse. What *was* the feeling . . . this queer new awareness of power? As if she could afford, now, to be generous about Lindy because she had up her sleeve some strange and terrible trump card . . . ?

What absurd tricks her mind was playing her tonight! I must be nearly delirious, she reflected, not without a touch of pride. Perhaps her temperature was even higher now—104°, perhaps, or even 105°? She wished she could take it again, just to satisfy her curiosity, but of course she couldn't possibly, not with Geoffrey standing there, waiting for her to set off to Lindy's on her errand. Cautiously but trying hard to seem just as usual, she began to negotiate the steep incline of the stairs.

The French windows at the back of Lindy's house opened at a push, as Geoffrey had said they would; and for a full minute Rosamund stood quite still on the threshold of the pitch dark room, smelling the Lindy smell. Newly-watered plants in their good earth; polish; and the faint exotic smell that might be almost anything from expensive chocolates to fresh flowers, and yet was always the same.

The darkness hung round her, chilling and yet somehow protective, and she felt a curious unwillingness to move. It seemed easier just to stand here, and concentrate on planning, in an absurdly laboured and painstaking fashion, the perfectly simple actions that she needed to perform. Feel her way across to the door. Find the light switch. Turn on the light. Look around by the telephone—on the mantelpiece—on the hall table—anywhere where Lindy might have propped a note for her sister to find when she came in.

And those are the only sorts of places we're entitled to look in for tonight, Rosamund found herself thinking. By tomorrow, of course, or the next day, when she still isn't back, we'll be searching through her desk, reading her letters, sorting out her papers for clues. . . . Suddenly the implications of her thoughts hit her. Why was she assuming, with such unquestioning certainty, that Lindy had really vanished? Absolutely all that had happened so far was that Lindy had for some reason failed to keep an appointment: was this a sufficient reason for supposing that they had some tragic mystery on their hands?

I must be half dreaming still, Rosamund told herself, forcing herself into movement, action; forcing herself to discipline her racing thoughts. Slowly, cautiously, balancing herself by one hand or the other against such shadowed, anonymous bits of furniture as loomed close, Rosamund began to move across the room towards the door, her footsteps almost silent on the carpet, her breath shallow as she picked her slow way through the blackness.

A sudden burst of movement, a rush of hurtling, indescribable sound brought her to a standstill with a gasp of terror; and then her terror disintegrated into shaky

laughter and a thumping heart as volley after volley of
ferocious yapping filled the darkness, echoing back and
forth off the walls, seeming to come from all directions at
once, so that it was hard to know where to step not to fall
over her vociferous little opponent.

But it was all right. Shang Low—whose talents were in
some directions not so very different from his mistress's—must have managed to combine this display of
reckless ferocity with a certain number of very sensible precautions against being trodden on, for Rosamund
managed to cross the last half of the room and turn on the
light without touching him at all. As she turned to face him
in the reassuring blaze of light, the infuriated little creature seemed to calm down a little. He was still barking, but
some of the shrillness of outrage had subsided. As Rosamund moved towards him, holding out her hand in spe-
cious friendship, he backed away, the barks subsiding to
a sort of high-pitched scolding, and then to a peevish,
intermittent growl, such as he had often favoured her with
in the past.

He was still suspicious, of course, and rightly so. He
followed her, not a foot behind, from door to telephone,
from telephone to mantelpiece, from mantelpiece to hall
table. A blank having been drawn in all these places, the
two with one accord turned to look at each other, as if to
say: What next?

The kitchen, of course, was a possibility. One might
very reasonably leave a note on the kitchen table with a
fair certainty of it being seen; so Rosamund, followed by
her baleful little bodyguard, proceeded thither. But to no
purpose; there was no note in sight. Nor had anything
been left cooking, or soaking, or drying up, to suggest
some unforeseen delay in the cook's return. Everything
was tidy as always, but not with that deathly tidiness
which means that the owner has really left home. After a
long, thoughtful survey, Rosamund and Shang Low moved
away, to stand and think once more in the hall.

Upstairs, perhaps? Rosamund remembered that occasionally, when Peter was very late, she would pin to his
pillow the note reminding him about his clean shirt, or his
dentist appointment, or whatever. Perhaps Lindy and her
sister followed the same custom?

She turned towards the stairs.

She had thought that she must already have witnessed the ultimate of Shang Low's potential as a guard dog; but nothing she had ever experienced or imagined could compare with the paroxysms of outrage and fury into which this small movement of hers threw him. He flung himself to the foot of the stairs, and with eyes popping, teeth bared, prepared to bar her path with every ounce of the strength and fury so tightly packed in his small, trembling body.

It was this pathetic smallness of his body, in contrast to the hugeness of his outrage, that made Rosamund pause. She hadn't the heart to break down his miniature but so gallant defence—a tiny Horatius guarding his great bridge all alone. Indeed, she really hadn't quite the courage, either: his fury was quite frightening, when you stood face to face with it like this. What was it all about, anyway? What was there upstairs that he must preserve from her with his very life?

Suddenly she felt too tired to bother. Her head ached too much. What was the point, anyway? Eileen would soon be home and could go and look; why, Lindy herself might be back any moment now. One way or another, everything would be explained in due course. What *were* they all making such a fuss about? Every minute she was finding it harder and harder to remember.

CHAPTER XIII

When she got home, Geoffrey was pacing about the sitting room. He looked up eagerly.

"Any luck?"

"No. Nothing. Well, there might have been something upstairs, but I couldn't go and look—Shang Low wouldn't let me. He just went mad, barking and snarling, when I tried to go up the stairs, so I gave up."

Geoffrey smiled briefly, not really listening.

"Oh, well." He paused in his pacing, frowned, and

slowly lowered himself on to the sofa, as though to think better in a sitting position.

"I'm just wondering," he said, "whether, possibly, there's been some sort of muddle about the time? That would explain everything. Though I did tell her, most clearly, that it was my late evening, and I wouldn't be able to meet her till after eight. . . . I wonder if she rang from home . . . ? Did you say you didn't see her *at all* today, Rosamund? Not this morning, or any time? Or hear her going out?"

Again the throbbing, the aching in her head when she tried to concentrate her thoughts. Had she seen Lindy? Well, of course she had, at that meeting at Norah's. . . . But that was *yesterday,* wasn't it, not today . . . ? Again confusion swept her thoughts, whirling them this way and that like a high wind. Sleeping all the afternoon got you so confused. . . .

"It *is* Tuesday, isn't it?" she asked Geoffrey. Then, seeing his expression, she hastily added: "I'm sorry— I'm being stupid. It's just that I'm so sleepy. . . ."

It was not exactly impatience that she saw clouding his face now; more a sort of withdrawal. She knew that he was hurt that she could just simply feel sleepy while he was still so anxious. By her ill-judged excuse she had destroyed for them that tentative sense of comradeship in anxiety that had so moved her a little while ago.

"Yes, it's Tuesday," he said, chilly and patient again. *"Do* try to be a help, darling. You can't really be as sleepy as all that. It's only half past ten."

"Yes. Yes, I know. I'm sorry. Just let me think a minute. I've been doing so many things today, I have to try and remember. . . ."

What things? Had she done anything at all? Well, of course she had. She'd washed up breakfast, tidied the house, got ready for Norah's coffee morning. . . . No, that was yesterday, Monday: she *must* try to keep it clear. Well, then, it must have been something else today . . . what did she usually do on Tuesdays?

Shopping? No, she hadn't gone shopping today, she felt sure. . . . No, of course she hadn't; she began to remember now, the fog had looked so thick, and her throat had been hurting. . . . Yes, that's right! That's how she'd spent the day—she'd been ill.

But what to tell Geoffrey? She couldn't—wouldn't—
plead illness at a time like this, particularly with him looking so aloof and peremptory, simply wanting facts out of
her. Brief, relevant facts, to help him to find Lindy. But he
won't find her, gloated the evil little voice inside her: and
somehow the fighting down of this little voice restored
courage and clarity.

"Well, I didn't go out at all, anyway," she said confidently, feeling that this, at least, was the truth. "I was
doing things about the house all day—you know. Tidying,
washing—things like that." She moved over to the fireplace
and sank into a chair facing her husband. It was an effort
not to close her eyes, so great was the relief of sitting
down.

She became aware of his eyes moving down her outstretched legs.

"Were you looking round the garden as well as the
house, when you went over to Lindy's just now?" he asked
curiously; and Rosamund, startled, followed the line of
his gaze. Her nearly new black court shoes were coated
with mud—thick, heavy, half-dried mud—with bits of grass
blades bedded in it. A sharp, agonised sense of—something
—passed through her head like a sudden pain, vanished
before she could grasp it, and left her as puzzled as Geoffrey. They both stared at the shoes in equal bewilderment.

"No. No, of course I didn't," said Rosamund, utterly
baffled. "I just went along the side path and across the bit
of concrete by the French window. I can't think how they
got like that." She stared at the two muddy feet in a concentrated yet unfocused way until they seemed no longer
to be her own. They seemed to swell, to shrink, to
glide away to an immense distance and then come scud-
ding back to fit on to her legs again. *Her* legs, yes, she
mustn't lose track of whose legs they were that had been
tramping through unknown mud to some unknown desti-
nation. But what on earth was Geoffrey thinking of this
long silence . . . ?

But it could only have been going on for a second or
two, after all. As she glanced at him, she saw that he had
stopped looking at her feet, had given up the problem.

"Oh, well . . ." he glanced at his watch, his mind moving restlessly forward. "Eileen should be here soon now,
I should think . . . she said an hour or so. . . ." He got up.

moved over to the window, and gazed for a long minute past the heavy curtain, carelessly thrust aside, into the street.

"The fog's definitely lifting," he announced, muffled, over his shoulder. "If she was held up anywhere by fog, she should be clear now. . . ." Rosamund, from the other side of the room, was aware of his eyes piercing and probing through the lessening obscurity, trying to force out of it the familiar, long-awaited figure. She could feel, locked inside him, waiting to leap forth, the smile, the wave, the rushing to the front door. . . .

I ought to tell him, she thought. It's not fair to let him go on waiting and hoping like this . . . and in the same instant realised that this thought was nonsensical. For she had nothing to tell. She knew no more than he did—less, in fact, for he, not she, had been the last one to have seen Lindy, the last one to have spoken to her.

"I suppose it *was* she who rang you up?" she heard herself asking; and wondered whatever could have put so idiotic an idea in her mind.

His head jerked back from behind the curtain. He stared at her.

"What on earth do you mean? Who else could it have been?"

He might well ask. Rosamund herself was wondering what she could possibly have meant. But she must go through with it now, think of something vaguely sensible, or else simply admit that she was light-headed with fever and be done with it. She thought of the dutifully-repressed annoyance with which he would greet such news at just this juncture: the clumsy, agonising attempts at a display of sympathy and concern at this addition—or rather interruption—to his worries. No, she couldn't face it.

"Who else *could* it have been?" he repeated.

"Well——" Rosamund thought quickly—"It only just crossed my mind, but supposing Eileen—after all, they *are* sisters, their voices may sound quite alike on the telephone. If *she* wanted to ask your advice about something, and took for granted you recognised her voice and so didn't bother to say who she was—could it have been that? After all, she might easily be wanting advice about her problems. You know—Basil and everything."

You could see that for one second Geoffrey was considering this bizarre possibility. But the flaws were glaring and obvious.

"Then why wouldn't she have said so, when I rang her up just now? Of course it wasn't her! Apart from the fact that *she* didn't turn up either. . . . It wouldn't explain anything whatever!"

No, it wouldn't. The snub—if snub you could call it from so anxious a man——was well deserved. Rosamund lapsed into silence, slumped deeper into her chair, and sensed rather than saw Geoffrey resuming his vigil behind the curtain.

She must have dozed off a little, for the next thing she knew Eileen was standing in the middle of the room, her pale hair glistening with damp and her face pinched with cold. She must have only just arrived, for she was still wearing a white belted mackintosh, and her whole presence still radiated that disruptive sense of outdoors suddenly brought in. But already she and Geoffrey were talking hard, both at once, as it seemed to Rosamund's half-awakened senses.

"No, Geoffrey, really, I don't know a thing!" Eileen was assuring him. "She didn't tell me she was going to ring you up, or meet you, or anything. I've just *no* idea what it could be about."

"And she hadn't told you anything about being worried? I mean—quite apart from whether she meant to consult me or not—was there anything you know of that she *could* have been worrying about?"

There was a tiny pause. Then Eileen laughed, a slightly forced sound.

"Can one ever say, of anyone, that there is *nothing* they could be worrying about? All I can say is, I don't know of anything *in particular*, just now."

She had the defensive look that she so often wore when Lindy was talking at her, teasing her about her orderliness or her sobriety. She looked uncomfortable, too, standing there in her mackintosh, as if about to go at any moment. Rosamund roused herself.

"Do sit down, Eileen," she urged. "Geoffrey, take her coat, will you?"—and after the little disturbance was over, and they were all seated, she told Eileen, a little apologetically, how she had been trespassing around hers and Lindy's house that evening.

"Though I must say Shang Low did heroic service in stopping me taking any liberties. I wouldn't like to be a burglar in your place, Eileen! Do you know, he just wouldn't let me set foot on the stairs. Anybody'd think you kept the Crown Jewels up there, or something!"

Eileen looked startled for a moment.

"Oh. Yes, well, he's like that," she explained. "He doesn't mind people in the places where he's accustomed to see them; it's only if they suddenly do something that they don't usually do, like you going upstairs. I expect you've never been upstairs in our house before, and that's why—— Incidentally, why *did* you go up? What did you think you'd find?"

Eileen's voice had changed, become quite sharp. Rosamund, in some confusion, explained her idea about the note on the bed.

"Oh. Oh, I see." Eileen seemed mollified. "No, Lindy would never have left a note there. She wouldn't have left a note at all, actually. She wouldn't expect me to be anxious, just not finding her in. We both go in and out as we please."

"But aren't you anxious, then?" put in Geoffrey eagerly. "You seemed as if you were, when I rang you up. But of course, if Lindy quite often does this sort of thing. . . ."

"It's not that. It's . . ." Eileen clasped her cold hands tightly together in her lap, as if to give herself courage. Then she looked Geoffrey full in the face.

"You've just asked me if I know of any reason why Lindy should be worried, and I've told you that I don't. But when you rang me up just now at Molly's, you didn't just say Linda sounded *worried*. You said she sounded *scared*. You haven't said that again, since I got here. Is it true?"

She looked both shy and aggressive. Geoffrey observed her in some surprise.

"Why, yes," he said. "Certainly it's true. I suppose I didn't repeat it again in exactly the same words because—well, I assumed, naturally . . ." His sentence petered our under Eileen's accusing gaze, and he started again. "Well, anyway, let's not quarrel about words. Let's begin again at the beginning. Do you know any reason why she should be *scared*?"

Eileen's gaze stayed on his face for a very long time

before she answered, or so it seemed to Rosamund. It seemed to her, too, that for some reason Eileen was having to bring to this interview every scrap of courage she possessed, summoning it up from every corner of her soul, in the desperate fear that even so it might not be quite enough for what she had to do.

"No," she answered Geoffrey steadily. "I don't know any reason. Do you?"

Now it was Geoffrey's turn to stare, but she did not flinch.

"There's something else, isn't there?" she persisted. "Something you haven't told me?"

"The girl has second sight!" exclaimed Geoffrey, with a not very successful attempt at lightening the tension. "Yes. There is, actually. I didn't tell you before—either of you—" (this with a glance at Rosamund) "because really it's so irrelevant. I'm sure it is, though I admit it shook me a little at the time. A little while after Lindy's call, while I was still at the office—more or less on my own, by then, you understand, I'm the only one who stays late on Tuesdays—the telephone went again. The switchboard girl had gone by then, of course, so I took it myself, and——"

"And it was Lindy again?" prompted Eileen eagerly. She was leaning forward in her chair.

"No. It was no one. No one at all."

"You mean no one answered—said anything?"

"Not a word. I kept saying Hullo and Press Button A, and things like that, but nothing happened . . . just a muddled sort of sound—you know—as if someone was messing about who didn't know how to work it . . . and then the receiver seemed to bang down at the other end, and that was the end of that."

"Well, I suppose it *was* someone not knowing how to work it," said Eileen, seizing on the idea. "It's always happening, especially since this new kind with all those pips and putting threepenny pieces in instead of pennies. Lots of people lose their nerve over them. Not Lindy, though. It couldn't have been *her*."

"No. I'm sure you're right, Eileen. Now that I'm looking back on it, I'm sure it must have been something quite commonplace like that. But at the time—I don't know how to describe it—but I had the feeling that the person messing about at the other end was in some sort of terrible

trouble . . . trying desperately to get through to me. If
I was a fanciful sort of fellow I'd have said there was
something almost telepathic about it—a sort of wordless
s.o.s. from one soul to another—but of course I don't believe in that sort of nonsense. But then, as time went on,
and she still didn't turn up . . . and then coming back and
finding the house all dark and shut-up looking . . . it all
seemed to hit me at once, if you can understand. . . ."

"And what do you think now?" asked Eileen, her eyes
fixed on him. For a few seconds they scanned each
other's faces tensely, as if for some clue, some sign, they
knew not what.

Then suddenly Geoffrey shrugged his shoulders, smiled.

"I think we're all getting a bit worked up," he declared. "It's my fault, I know—I don't know why I
should have panicked like that all about nothing. I daresay Lindy'll be along any minute now, with some
rational explanation. Meanwhile, let's all have a drink,
and then go to bed. What will you have, Eileen? Sherry or
gin?" He moved towards the cupboard. He had forgotten, evidently, that Eileen didn't drink.

She didn't remind him. She just grinned, a little awkwardly, looking suddenly like a schoolgirl, with childlike
smudges of tiredness under her eyes.

"No—no thanks. I don't think so. I ought to be going,
really."

She got up, and Rosamund, dazed with headache, did not
press her to stay. There seemed nothing more to be
said by any of them; the whole problem seemed to become more and more vague, and futile, and pointless,
the more they discussed it. She pulled herself out of the
chair and walked out of the room to see Eileen off at the
front door. She did not notice that the mud, now dry and
brittle, was flaking off her shoes at every step. Indeed,
when she came back and saw the little dark lumps and
blobs all across the sitting room floor she couldn't think,
for the minute, what they could possibly be.

CHAPTER XIV

The emotional laws of probability are quite different from the mathematical ones. More often than not it happens, when some disaster threatens, that as the odds against a happy outcome mount, so, by some healing mechanism of the mind, does the optimism of the victim. Thus it came about that Geoffrey, who the previous night had seemed unable to conceive of anything at all to account for Lindy's having disappeared for a single evening, was this morning able to think of a dozen perfectly satisfactory explanations for her having disappeared for the night as well.

Eileen had dashed in before leaving for work with the news that Lindy still had not returned. It was Geoffrey who answered the door to her, and from upstairs in the bedroom Rosamund could hear their voices rising and falling in reassuring cadences as they vied with each other in plausible explanations. That Lindy had perhaps left a message with some careless neighbour who had failed to deliver it? That she had been trying to ring all the evening, but something had been wrong with the line? That she had got stranded somehow, at some party or something? They bandied the suggestions back and forth like skilled players at some ball game, neither of them fumbling or letting the ball drop, until by mutual consent they counted the game over and put the ball away in a safe place: namely, in the comfortable conclusions that there would no doubt be a message for Geoffrey at the office—for Eileen at the shop. Meantime Rosamund, being on the spot, must look after Shang Low. Geoffrey came back upstairs swinging the keys of next door on his little finger quite cheerfully.

"You don't mind, do you, Rosamund," he asked—stated, rather, such was his easy confidence in her co-operation. "Just take him up the road a couple of times, and if no one's back by lunch time, then give him a tin of the Doggo-Whatsit. He doesn't terribly like it, Eileen says, but it'll do until Lindy comes back."

But she won't come back, Rosamund was thinking dully. I'll have to feed him tomorrow, too. And the next day, and the day after that, for evermore, or until they decide to give away the dog. How long will that be? How soon do people give up hope?

"Of course. I'll see to it," she said mechanically, longing for Geoffrey to go so that she could get back into bed. All she wanted to do was to lie there and doze away the hours until the headache and the lassitude left her, which surely must be quite soon. One-day flu, they were calling it this season, and why should *she* get it worse than anyone else? As soon as Geoffrey was gone she'd go and ask the Dawsons to see to the dog; they'd very likely enjoy it, one or both of them, especially if it turned out a nice day.

It wasn't a particularly nice day, but the fog was nearly gone, and Mrs Dawson seemed quite willing to undertake the small chore. Naturally enough, she accepted without question that Lindy was away for a day or two; and now, having handed over the keys and cleared the kitchen with weary incompetence, Rosamund felt free to crawl thankfully back into the unmade bed. She lay, eyes closed, thinking about the things she hadn't done. The washing was piling up, and the bath hadn't been cleaned —lots of things—but they could wait till tomorrow. Tomorrow she would be better. By tomorrow it would be clear that——

Clear that what? Rosamund realised that she must have fallen asleep in the middle of her thought, for now she could see that the morning was already far advanced, with the winter sun struggling towards its feeble zenith and filling the untidy bedroom with a late, unnerving brightness.

And the telephone was ringing. She scrambled out of bed, thrust her feet into her slippers, and was half way down the stairs before the dizziness of sudden movement caught up with her. There she was obliged to stand for a moment, clutching the banisters while the expected blackness broke over her, receded; then she proceeded on her way, amazed, really, that the telephone was still ringing, for all this seemed to have taken a very long time.

"Hullo?" she said hoarsely, holding the receiver closer to her ear; and again: "Hullo?" She knew by now that

there was going to be no answer, nothing but the faintly
breathing silence: but just once more she said "Hullo?"
and straightaway heard the click of the receiver being
replaced at the other end.

It was partly her own fault, of course; she should have
given her number, as you are supposed to do; or said
"This is Rosamund Fielding speaking" or "Press Button
A", or something like that. She hadn't been in the least
helpful towards her ghostly caller.

Never mind. There wasn't anything she at all wanted
to hear, not while her head was still aching like this. She
didn't even want to hear about Lindy—that she was back,
or wasn't back: to Rosamund's present way of feeling
both messages would have exactly the same significance;
namely, that she would have to get dressed and do something. So indeed would any other message that she could
think of . . . the coalman about to deliver half a ton of
anthracite . . . a dear old friend up in London for the day
and free to come round just at lunch time. . . . Feeling
nothing but relief, Rosamund put the receiver back and
went back thankfully upstairs.

Twice—three times—during her long, long sleep that
day Rosamund fancied she heard the telephone ringing,
but never forcefully enough to rouse her. Rather it
merged into her uneasy dreams, into her half-sleeping
awareness of headache and discomfort. It was the headache itself that seemed to be ringing through the house,
remorselessly, over and over again. If only it would keep
still, stay inside her head, and not keep rampaging and
ringing down there, then it wouldn't hurt so much.

And at last it all stopped. She fell into a dreamless
sleep, and when she woke she knew at once that she was
recovering. The pain was nearly gone, her mind was
clear, and she knew without taking it that her temperature was down.

But once again it was evening; once again she had
slept all day, right into the darkness. But it wasn't as
late as it had been when she woke up yesterday; it was
only half past five. There was a whole hour before Geoffrey
would be home—or Peter either; it was orchestra practice tonight. Now that she was better she must exert herself to make things comfortable as usual for their return,

think of something nice to cook for supper in spite of a
larder nearly bare after two days of no shopping.

Thinking hard about eggs, tins of soup, rice, that sort
of thing, Rosamund dressed quickly, though a little shak-
ily, and at the end was once more confronted by those
mysteriously muddy shoes. Tonight, in a hurry to get
supper on, she was inclined to regard them less as a
mystery than as a nuisance. No time to clean them now.
She pushed them out of the way, and began hastily looking for another pair. The room was in a dreadful muddle after its two days of neglect; there seemed to be shoes
and clothes everywhere; even her outdoor coat, for some
reason, was lying on the floor by the bed—had been, she
remembered, ever since last night.

Feeling strong enough, now, to bother about such
things, she bent to pick it up, and was surprised to find
that it was quite damp. Yes, and streaked with mud . . .
but her dawning puzzlement at this was a moment later
utterly obliterated by a discovery so bewildering that she
could only drop back onto the edge of the bed and stare
helplessly. For as she lifted the coat, shaking it a little
to remedy its crumpled state, a largish object thumped
to the floor and lay there, inert and inexplicable.

Lindy's handbag.

Scarlet, and brand new, and shining it had been when
Rosamund had last seen it. . . . "A Christmas present
to myself!" Lindy had exclaimed exuberantly, only last
weekend, as she proudly exhibited all its cunning zips and
pockets. "It was so exactly what I wanted, I couldn't bear
to leave it and just hope that someone would buy it for
me—I just *knew* they wouldn't, poor me! I thought of
buying it for Eileen, but then I thought *no,* Eileen would
much rather have a plain brown one to match her suit,
wouldn't you, Eileen . . . ?"

Rosamund could almost imagine that Lindy was in
the room talking to her now, so clearly did the scene, the
whole feel of it, come back to her as she sat foolishly
staring. But Lindy was gone, disappeared, and here was
the gorgeous new bag, but new no longer. Now it lay
limp and battered, covered with scratches, the handle
half wrenched off, the gold of the clasps dulled. As if years
had passed since last weekend, not a mere three days. . . .

"They stole little Bridget
    For seven years long;
And when she came home again
    Her friends were all gone."

The words wandered idiotically through Rosamund's
mind. In that first, stupefying moment, the notion that
Lindy had been stolen away by fairies, and that Rosamund herself had been lying in an enchanted sleep,
seemed no more unlikely than any other imaginable
explanation of it all. How else could the new bag have
suffered half a bag-lifetime of wear and tear since she
last saw it? But now she bent forward, picked it up and
examined it in the ordinary light of reason.

No, this wasn't the wear and tear of mysteriously lost
years; this was some sudden, disastrous accident. The
bag had been dragged at—wrenched—pulled through briars
—flung among sharp stones . . . the kind of damage it could
be expected to suffer if it had hurtled headlong down some
jagged cliff in its owner's clutching hand. . . .

Rosamund felt a thundering in her head. For the first
time she was confronted, inescapably, by the sheer, staggering coincidence of her dream. Why should she have
dreamed—and so vividly, too—of pushing Lindy over a
cliff on just the evening when Lindy disappeared? And
whence the muddy shoes? And the coat? And now the
handbag? Slowly, hardly knowing what she expected to
find, Rosamund opened the bag and looked inside.

Now she knew what she had expected—hoped, rather.
She had hoped—without quite knowing why—that the bag
would be empty, a discarded shell, as empty of evidence
as everything else in this whole mysterious business. To
find it fully equipped with all the usual contents of a
handbag—comb, purse, powder compact, cheque book,
library ticket, several neatly folded pound notes in an
inside compartment—to find all this seemed to Rosamund
to constitute a terrible confirmation of her half-acknowl-
edged fears.

For this, surely, must mean that Lindy had met with
some disaster? How should she have stayed away for
nearly two days without money, cheque book, anything
at all? Without them she could not have spent the night in
any hotel, bought herself any meals, or travelled on

train or bus to get to friends. No woman could possibly leave home for any purpose, good or ill, sensible or foolish, without taking her handbag.

No, Lindy must certainly have set out with her handbag —new still, bright and shining—when she left home yesterday; but who was it who had brought it back, last night, damp and battered, and flung it carelessly on Rosamund's bedroom floor? Again the dream-wind whistled through her mind, the thunder of the dream-seas broke over her. She remembered the triumph she had felt in her merciless dream-soul as she watched Lindy's white face hurtling to its doom. . . .

Was it indeed possible that this had been no dream? She had had a temperature yesterday. Could it during the afternoon have become high enough for delirium? And if so, could one, in delirium, lure a hated enemy to some deserted cliff, push her over it, and come home again with no memory of it all except in the form of a dream?

Even if one could, there still seemed a hundred objections. One by one Rosamund summoned them up, examined them, and handed them over to her trembling soul for its comfort. First of all, it was no easy matter getting from here to the coast—two hours at least by train. And first you'd have to look up the trains, get to the main line station, buy a ticket—if you were ill enough to be delirious, would you possibly be able to manage all these fairly exacting activities? And even then, the train wouldn't take you straight to some conveniently deserted cliff top just suitable for murder; it would take you to the station on the outskirts of some seaside resort. You would then have to find a bus—make your way through an unfamiliar town, through its miles of peripheral bungalows and guest-houses—find your way to the cliffs, if any, choose a bit that wasn't covered with bandstands and bathing huts and things—all this in the pitch dark, and with limbs and will-power as weak and unserviceable as they would certainly be if you were ill enough for delirium. And—biggest complication of all—you'd have to have Lindy trailing obligingly along with you all this time, without sense or explanation. "Well, you see, I want to find a cliff to push you over when no one's looking" would hardly be a sufficient inducement.

Obviously, it was impossible.

And yet, impossible or not, there they *were*; the bag, the muddy shoes, the coat. Inanimate, merciless, immune to argument, they were there, in front of her. It was no use telling *them* that it was impossible. . . .

For a moment, the solution seemed temptingly simple. She was stronger, after all, than these inanimate accusers, simply by virtue of being alive while they were not. All she had to do was to wash the mud off the shoes, polish them well; hang up the coat till it was thoroughly dry and then brush it; put Lindy's handbag into Lindy's house, where it belonged: and then there would be no mystery left to puzzle over. Nothing at all.

She realised, of course, with the intellectual part of her mind, that what this amounted to was a criminal tampering with the evidence; a bare-faced suppressing of clues; but that wasn't what it *felt* like at all. It felt like simply putting everything right again. Suddenly she understood exactly how it is that liars and cheats so often manage to retain their self-respect—genuinely to retain it. They are not trying to take advantage of anybody or to escape anything; they are simply trying to make their original misfortune of misdemeanour not have happened.

But before she had time to act on her ostrich-like impulse—or to reject it either—a ring on the front door bell threw her into total panic. Without any thought at all she thrust the handbag out of sight into the wardrobe and rushed downstairs.

She could not have said what it was that she was afraid of seeing when she opened the front door. A policeman with a warrant for her arrest? Lindy's avenging spirit, transparent, in clanking chains? It was no wonder that Carlotta took a small step backwards and stared at her.

"I say! Goodness! Are you ill, or something?"

"No. Oh no! That is, I think I've had a touch of 'flu, but it's getting better. . . . I'm all right now. Do come in. We're in a bit of a mess, I'm afraid. . . ." Rosamund talked on, at random, trying to recover herself; and by the time she had Carlotta settled in the sitting room she could feel that her face was looking ordinary again, or fairly so.

"Well, thanks a lot," said Carlotta, relaxing pleasurably into the easy chair that Rosamund had pulled

forward for her. "I haven't come to stay, really, you
know: got to get back to the brood." In referring to her
family Carlotta always chose phrases, half-humorously,
which made her four children sound both more nu-
merous and a good deal younger than they really were, a
crowd of faceless tots milling round the skirts of the
Mother Figure. "I just popped in with a message from
your husband, actually . . . he seemed worried. He's
been trying to ring you all the afternoon, it seems, and
couldn't get any answer, so in the end he rang us."

"But why? What's happened?"

It would be about Lindy, of course. The possibility that
she had been found now seemed just as terrifying as the
possibility that she hadn't.

Carlotta looked surprised.

"Happened? Nothing, that I know of. He only wanted
to let you know that he'd be late home tonight. That's all.
He must be a very considerate man, your Geoffrey. Lots
of husbands wouldn't ring at all, let alone go to all this
trouble about it. My goodness, though, you do look washed
out. Is it the 'flu? Did you have it very badly?"

The sudden sympathy quite broke down Rosamund's
determination not to let anyone know how ill she had
been feeling these last two days. Not to let Geoffrey know,
really—that was the main thing; what was the harm in
telling Carlotta? Besides, what other explanation could
she give for her evidently strange appearance?

"Yes, I suppose it is," she admitted. "It's this one-day
'flu that everyone's been having, though it's lasted two
days with me. My temperature was a hundred and two
last night," she added, warming to the recital.

Carlotta leaned forward, frowning anxiously. You might
have supposed that the anxiety was for her neighbour's
state of health, but even Rosamund could tell that this
wasn't so. Carlotta was in fact being agonisingly torn
between two treasured, but sadly contradictory, images
of herself: one, as the woman who is never ill; the
second, as the woman who had had a higher temperature than anybody else, ever, and *much* higher than
Rosamund's palty 102°. The second image won, by a
short head, and Rosamund was soon listening to a colourful account of the measles epidemic that had struck
Carlotta's household five years ago. With a temperature of

a hundred and five herself, she had yet managed to nurse her "whole nursery full of kids" day and night, without any assistance from anyone. You didn't get the impression that her husband had helped at all—or even that he had selfishly left it all to her; he simply didn't come into the story at all, though of course he must have been there at the time, in some corner of the house or other.

As the story proceeded, it occurred to Rosamund that here was her chance to get some first-hand information.

"But weren't you delirious some of the time, with a temperature as high as that?" she asked disingenuously. "Did you find yourself doing silly things—forgetting what you were doing—anything like that?"

You could see that Carlotta loved being asked this question; she was rolling it round her mind, savouring it, like a connoisseur of wines, before answering:

"Well . . . you know, I've sometimes thought since that I must have been. It was very strange, the night when Jeremy was at his worst—his temperature was about a hundred and two, I remember, and mine was touching a hundred and six, and he kept calling for drinks, poor little kid. And every time I went down to the kitchen I had a queer feeling that I was *floating* there: not walking at all, but just floating down the stairs and across the hall. . . ." She made faint little flapping movements with her arms to illustrate this remarkable sensation, and her dark eyes were wide with self-admiration.

"And did you ever find that you'd just been dreaming—that you hadn't fetched him the drink at all, when you thought you had?" persisted Rosamund, bent on making the most of her captive informant.

"Oh no!" Carlotta seemed a little huffy. "No, I never let the child down once, no matter how ill I felt. Somehow I managed to keep going, see to everything, the whole crowd of them all needing attention all the time. I never let up all that night . . . the doctor said it was a wonder I hadn't died, working all day and all night with a temperature like that! He said he'd never heard of anything like it . . . !"

Neither had Rosamund. And so the conversation continued—necessarily rather at cross-purposes, with Rosamund's determination to extract technical information for ever tangling with Carlotta's determination to pre-

sent her own heroism as the main point of the discourse.
All that Rosamund could gather in the end was that
while a very high temperature might no doubt make *some*
people go to pieces and do silly things, it could never
possibly have that effect on Carlotta; and the following
prolonged exposition of all the remarkable qualities in Carlotta that made this the case precluded all hope of getting
any further information out of her. And eventually the
call of the Brood (combined, perhaps, with the fast-
accumulating evidence that Rosamund had no intention at
all of asking her to stay to supper) induced Carlotta to
take her leave.

CHAPTER XV

After she had closed the door on Carlotta, Rosamund
came slowly back into the sitting room, and it dawned on
her that she was probably going to spend the rest of the
evening in solitude. Geoffrey had said he would be late—
and no doubt he meant very late, or he wouldn't have gone
to so much trouble to make sure she got the message. And
Peter still wasn't back, which probably meant he had
gone off somewhere with a crowd of his friends straight
after orchestra practice. Quite soon, he either would
or wouldn't ring up to say he either was or wasn't coming
home for supper, which he then either would or wouldn't
do. It was no good trying to plan anything round Peter's
activities.

Rosamund was rather glad on the whole of the prospect of being on her own. For one thing, she now
wouldn't have to set her wits to work on all that rice
and stuff. She could simply go back to bed, if she chose, for
all the rest of the evening.

But, rather to her surprise, she no longer felt like lying
down. On the contrary, she felt restless, full of uneasy
energy; and above all, she wanted to get out of this
house. Out—right away from the wearying mystery of the
shoes, and Lindy's wretched handbag; from the endless

telephone calls (although she hadn't answered them); and from her own profitless brooding. She would go out for a walk, that's what she would do, and when she came back perhaps she would find everything settled and ordinary again.

But where to walk to? What for? It seemed silly to go for a walk all by oneself—quite different from those evening strolls that she and Geoffrey had once enjoyed. She stood on the front step, hesitating, and feeling quite absurdly conspicuous. Going for a *walk?* All by *herself?* Where's her husband? . . . She felt the idle, imaginary comments flitting like bats up and down the dark road—winter bats, imaginary bats, for real bats are summer creatures, deep in hibernation in this season of the long nights and the deep, damp cold.

She shivered, nearly turned back indoors again, and then had an inspiration.

Shang Low. *That* would be an excuse for a walk, would give it a purpose. Since Eileen didn't seem to be back yet, to judge from the darkened windows, it was positively Rosamund's duty to take him for a walk—if he'd come with her, that is: she was never quite sure how deep the enmity between them might go.

But Shang Low was not one to let his enmities interfere with his pleasures. After his long day of solitude, broken only by two short strolls with Mr Dawson, and a tin of Doggo-loaf or some such substance (of which, Rosamund observed, he had not touched one mouthful), he allowed her, with enormous condescension, to fix his lead on to his collar and escort him out into the December night.

Slowly they moved together through the deserted roads. Now that she was on her feet, Rosamund realised that her feeling of restless returning energy had been something of an illusion. Her head was aching again, quite badly now, and she was already tired. She decided to go no farther than the railway bridge beyond the cricket ground. From there, she could go down the steps to the fenced footpath that ran alongside the line, and come home that way. There it would be safe to let Shang Low go free for a bit, with no risk from cars.

"Hullo. Good evening!"

The unknown male voice out of the darkness made

Rosamund jump; she hadn't noticed anyone approaching.

"Good evening," she responded warily, tugging at Shang Low's lead, trying to get him to co-operate in passing the stranger at a dignified and unhesitating pace. But Shang Low had found a particularly luscious bit of jutting out brickwork, and wasn't going to be parted from it till he had sniffed his fill, so Rosamund could only stand still and wait for him.

"It *is* you, isn't it?" the voice enquired, rather unhelpfully; and for a second the two stood peering into each other's faces in the darkness. Rosamund was racking her brains trying to place this vaguely familiar voice, this pale, rather pointed young face.

"Basil!" she exclaimed. "I didn't recognise you for a moment. How are you? Are you on your way to Li——?"

But Lindy wasn't there. Lindy might at this very moment be dead. She was at a loss how to finish her ill-conceived sentence.

"Well, to see *about* Lindy, you might say," he amended. "I hear there's a spot of bother going on. Eileen rang and told me—she's a plucky kid, you know," he digressed wonderingly. "I never thought she'd have the guts to ring me up after the flaming row we had; not about *anything*. She always used to be so scared, it was always *I* who had to make the first move after a bust-up. . . . She seems more mature, somehow, without being . . ."

It was clear that Basil would go on with these irrelevant and surely not very momentous speculations for as long as Rosamund cared to stand there listening to him; so she hard-heartedly brought him back to the point.

"Yes, we're all *awfully* worried about Lindy," she said. "No one can imagine what's happened. I suppose nothing new has turned up? Eileen hasn't heard anything?"

"Nope. I just thought I'd drop round, see if a strong right arm was needed, or any of that lark. In case I could do anything to help—" he finished, rather weakly. Rosamund found Basil's unpredictable swings from jauntiness to a sort of little-boy uncertainty rather appealing. She could see how Eileen could have fallen in love with him, and also how she could have found him impossible to live with.

"I should think there might be a lot you could do," she agreed. "Giving Eileen moral support, for a start. And then, if Lindy still doesn't turn up, I suppose, sooner or later, someone'll have to notify the police."

As she said it, the words gave her an unexpected little stab of fear; and it must have had the same effect on Basil, for he started.

"The *police?* Why—you don't think——?"

"No, of course not!" Rosamund wished very much that she had not raised the question. "I just meant, that if she goes on not turning up—well—I mean, we'll have to do *something.*"

Basil was frowning down at the faintly glistening pavement. He seemed as if many and complicated thoughts were surging through his head, and he was selecting, ordering, arranging them before trusting himself to speak again.

"Mrs Fielding," he said at last, "I think you and I should have a talk about all this *before* I go and see Eileen. May I walk along with you for a bit? Tell me what you know, from your vantage point just across the fence."

Rosamund began to comply; but by the time she had carefully left out all her own secret anxieties, there didn't seem much left to tell. She began asking him questions instead.

"Tell me," she said. "You've known Lindy for much longer than we have—— Is she the sort of person who might do something like this quite casually and irresponsibly? Just disappear for fun—for a whim—just because she felt like it? I'm asking, because my husband was suggesting something of the sort. He says that perhaps, since she's such a happy-go-lucky, unworrying sort of person herself, she might expect everyone else to be the same. It might not occur to her, he says, that we'd all be anxious."

"Is that what your husband says? He's really fallen for all that? Really and truly?"

What did he mean? It sounded so much as if he shared Rosamund's own private assessment of Lindy's character that she longed for him to elaborate.

"*Is* she the worrying type then, really? All this carefree light-heartedness—do you mean it's just an act? I'm sorry—I make her sound an absolute hypocrite!" she apologised hastily.

"Of course you do. Because that's what you think she is," observed Basil. "But never mind. After all, what *is* a hypocrite, when all's said and done? It's a person who pretends to have all sorts of kind and good feelings that he hasn't got. But what *should* such a person do—I'm asking you? Through no fault of his own, he just hasn't got these feelings—what ought he to do about it? Go on, tell me!"

Rosamund didn't tell him, of course, because it was so overwhelmingly clear that he intended to tell her. So she said nothing, and sure enough he proceeded:

"Hypocrites, as you call them, are simply people who are honestly trying to make good their emotional deficiencies. They are cultivating the best substitutes for actual feeling that they can possibly contrive. Is this wicked? Is a blind man wicked when he trains himself to behave normally by cultivating as best he can all sorts of substitutes for sight? Is a cripple wicked if . . ."

Basil's eloquence was once again carrying them far from the real point of their conversation. Rosamund interrupted him.

"But do tell me—from what you know of her—*would* Lindy just disappear like this? Might she? Is it in character?"

"Well." Basil was walking slower and slower as he pondered. "I don't think you know what a difficult question you're asking me. The fact that I've known her quite a long time makes it harder, not easier——" He came almost to a standstill, and Rosamund paused with him. Shang Low gave a censorious little sigh and waited.

"What would you say," suddenly burst out Basil. "If I told you that a few years ago, Lindy was quite, quite different from what she is now? Plain. Frumpish. Shy. Never went anywhere or did anything?"

"Well, I'd be very surprised. Naturally. Because she's so very attractive now, isn't she."

"You'd say so?" Basil was being so ostentatiously non-committal that Rosamund glanced at him enquiringly.

"In the faces of some very old ladies," Basil continued, apparently at a tangent. "You can still see traces of great beauty. In Lindy's face, if you look carefully, you can still see traces of great plainness."

Rosamund did not know what to say. Basil's revelations —if revelations they were, and not merely the unfounded guesses of one rather opinionated young man—were startling to her in the extreme. Forty-eight hours ago they would have seemed wholly delightful—a welcome confirmation of her own secret opinion that Lindy's charm and sociability were all part of an act. Under the present shadow of Lindy's disappearance they naturally could not be delightful in the same way—but even so, why should they make Rosamund feel so uneasy, so strange? They had reached the railway bridge now, and as Rosamund stared over the parapet towards the station lights, haloed in mist, she began to feel herself trembling. Basil was still speaking, describing the occasion when, as an undergraduate, he had first met Lindy—how withdrawn she had seemed, how shy—and with every sentence, Rosamund felt her fear growing. But why? Why should the story of Lindy's changing personality seem so sinister, so fraught with nightmare, unreasoning terror? It was as if some terrible memory had been awakened, deep inside her; with every word that Basil spoke, with every passing second, some fearful knowledge seemed to be ploughing its way up through thick layers of forgetfulness . . . up, up, relentlessly, towards her consciousness. How her limbs were shuddering . . . the very ground beneath her feet seemed to have caught the vibration, to be trembling, quivering, in exact rhythm with her fear.

"The bridge is shaking!" she cried out, the words forced from her involuntarily by the mounting sense of approaching revelation, the thunder of approaching fear. . . .

"Well, of course it is; there's a train coming." Basil glanced at her, puzzled by the tone of her voice.

"Of course; how silly!" She forced herself to answer, even to laugh a little as the roar of the coming train half swamped her consciousness, the thunder of sound, the blaze of sparks . . . and then it had passed . . . and with it passed that fearful sense of impending revelation. Her whole consciousness seemed to throb with relief as the memory, whatever it was, withdrew, and sank away, down, down, back into the depths from which it came.

"Let's not go along the railway path, let's go back by the road," begged Rosamund, trying to keep the trembling out of her voice. "It's quicker."

"Is it? O.K." Basil turned back on their tracks readily enough. She was thankful that he did not query her change of plan, or seem in the least bit interested in the reasons for it. For she could not possibly explain them to him—or indeed to herself. She was simply aware of an overwhelming and totally irrational terror at the prospect of going down those steps and along that little, narrow fenced-in path that led into the main road.

They walked home more quickly than they had come, talking, as if by mutual consent, of trivialities. Only when they reached Rosamund's gate did they speak again of the avowed reason for Basil's visit.

"Oh dear! It looks as if Eileen still isn't in," said Rosamund, looking up at the blank, black windows of the next door house. "What would you like to do? Would you like to come in and wait at our place for a bit, till she comes?"

"Well—no—— Thanks very much," said Basil. "It's very kind of you, but if you don't mind I'd rather wait at Eileen's. I'd like to be there when she comes in. . . . *You* know—"

So she handed the keys over to Basil, and Shang Low too; and then she let herself into the darkness of her home and closed the front door behind her.

CHAPTER XVI

And once again, the telephone was ringing. As she closed the front door and fumbled her way through the darkness to the light switch, Rosamund had time to feel sure that it was Geoffrey, and then to feel sure that it wasn't. She could not tell how long ago the ringing had started, but anyway it must have been just too long, for as she reached out her hand towards the instrument, it stopped. At that, she felt sure all over again that it *was* Geoffrey. How anxious he seemed to get in touch with her this evening! Had something happened? Some news of

Lindy, good or bad? Was that what was keeping him out late? Rosamund reflected that Eileen, too, was late: had they both heard of some news? No doubt this was why the telephone had been going all the afternoon—one or both of them trying to tell her about it. If only she had roused herself sufficiently to answer at least one of those neglected calls! She went upstairs and to bed determined to leap out again immediately, however sleepy she might be, at the very first ping of the telephone bell.

Not that she expected to go to sleep very soon, anyway; it was only a quarter to ten. But once in bed, she found that the three aspirins she had taken had not only dulled the headache, but seemed to have filled her whole body with drowsiness, particularly her eyes . . . the print of her library book, which she had taken with her to read, was dancing before her eyes, and she could not make out at all where she had got to in it. She knew that she had started the book already, two or three days ago, but it seemed impossible to find her place. She was puzzled, for it was a perfectly ordinary novel, not significant in any way—everyone knows that the more significant a book, the harder it is to find your place in it. She found it difficult even to recall who the characters were—was Evelyn a man or a woman? The whole book seemed to be about Evelyn and his—no, her—disagreeable mother . . . funny that she couldn't recollect one single thing about either of them.

She was too sleepy, that was the trouble; but all the same, she mustn't fall asleep and risk missing the telephone bell. *Telephone,* she said to herself severely, as her vision swam into sleep, and her eyes closed. . . . I *must* wake up if the telephone goes again. . . .

But it was not the telephone that broke into her dreams. Rosamund did not know how long she had been lying there, in a light, uneasy sleep, before she became aware that someone was looking at her. It was not a sudden awareness—she had no feeling of having been woken by any sound or movement; it was just a gradual, growing consciousness of being watched. At first, this did not seem to her an extraordinary thing. As she lay there, on the very edge of waking, she accepted the fact of being watched simply as one more of the facts that she knew about the familiar world that lay, so near and yet so inaccessi-

ble, just beyond the border-line of sleep. She knew quite
well that she herself was lying in this familiar world;
that the bedside light was still on, shining down on her,
showing up her sleeping face, her fast-closed eyes, to the
watcher by the bed. The watcher, she knew, was bending
over, was examining her face with silent intentness from
only a foot or two away; and she knew, without surprise,
that the watcher had been standing exactly thus for a long
time. For minutes? Seconds? Fractions of seconds? How
can one measure the long, long tracts of time that stretch
from dream to dream and back and forth along the wind-
ing boundaries of sleep?

In sudden terror, Rosamund awoke. There was a flurry
of movement, of sound, as she started up from her pillows;
as the library book thumped to the floor; as her hands,
released from nightmare, clutched convulsively at the
slipping blankets. Her eyes were open at last—she was
awake—her glance swept the room; but already there was
no one there.

Had there been anyone? In every bone, in every inch
of her flesh Rosamund knew that there had; but her
brain, ready and eager as brains always are to introduce doubt where none was, began at once to speculate
on the deceptive nature of nightmare. Though it hadn't
been a nightmare, exactly, for until the very moment
of waking she had felt no fear. Until then, she had been
held fast in the bonds of senseless unsurprise, of unreasoning acquiescence, as paralysing as the bonds of sleep
itself. The shock, the terror, the racing unanswered ques-
tionings, had come only with full awakening.

Had it perhaps been Geoffrey, trying not to wake her?
Her bones, her flesh, already knew that it hadn't, and even
her questing brain accepted it quite quickly. It just isn't
possible for a woman who has been married for eighteen
years not to know exactly what it sounds like when her
husband is trying not to wake her. Nor could it have
been Peter. He wouldn't have come in here to seek her
out unless it was something really important, like could
he finish all those cold sausages and the rest of the apple
pie; and if it was as important as that, then he would never
have crept considerately away without having extracted
a favourable answer.

How late was it? Rosamund looked at her little clock

and was surprised to find that it was only twenty-five to eleven. She felt as if she had slept so long—as if so much had happened—since she had last looked, and it had said quarter past ten. Reassured by the earliness of the hour —by the comfortable feeling that everyone up and down the road was still awake—she got out of bed, put on her dressing gown and slippers, and prepared to search the house.

Nothing. Nobody. Four rooms upstairs, three down—it didn't take long to ascertain that they were all empty, and all pretty much as she had last seen them. You would have to be a much more meticulous housewife than Rosamund to be able to say with certainty that those battered magazines hadn't been piled on the piano stool before; that two pairs of gloves and Peter's old scarf hadn't been spilling out of their usual repository in the hall chest; that the lid and the bottom drawer of Geoffrey's desk hadn't been open all along.

Rosamund shrugged. Fear cannot live on nothing. Confronted by this total lack of supporting evidence, it could only wither away. A clamour of young voices, girls and boys, swung by; the next door people but two were bidding loud goodbyes to some talkative and unhurried friends who seemed to be having trouble making their car start. Everywhere people were awake, friendly, accessible; you couldn't really go on feeling frightened. Rosamund exercised caution so far as to lock the back door—a thing she didn't usually do when Peter was out, because he had nearly always forgotten his key, and would drag them out of bed by knocking and ringing at some fearful hour; but it couldn't be helped. Having done that, she felt perfectly safe and reassured; so much so that when she came back in to her bedroom, she didn't notice anything different about it. She got back into bed and settled herself for sleep still without any notion that something had happened.

CHAPTER XVII

Rosamund never knew what time Geoffrey had come in that night. He had not woken her, and she had no consciousness—or at least no recollection—of his arrival. When she woke in the morning he was already up and dressed. As soon as he heard her stirring, he came over from the window and sat on the edge of the bed.

"Rosamund," he said, grave and puzzled. "Why didn't you *tell* me that Lindy meant to go down to Mother's the day before yesterday? I kept asking you if you knew anything about what she'd been doing."

"The day before yesterday?" Rosamund sat up, blinking stupidly, and trying to collect her thoughts. Don't look at me like that, she nearly added, but could you blame him, when she kept being so blank and useless whenever he asked her anything? Just as if she was *trying* to obstruct and slow down all his efforts to solve this unhappy mystery.

"I'm sorry—I'm just trying to sort out the days. She went down to Mother's on *Monday,* I know—I remember she left Norah's coffee morning early to finish some typing before she went. But you knew that, Geoffrey! You saw her that same evening. That was *before* all that—"

"No, Rosamund." Never, in all their married life, had his voice sounded like this when he spoke to her. "No, she didn't go that afternoon, it was too foggy. She told me that she'd had to ring up Mother and put it off. But she didn't say anything to me about going on Tuesday instead."

"Well, she didn't to me, either," said Rosamund, rather crossly. "I didn't even know that she'd cancelled the Monday time. *You* seem to know much more about it all than I do!"

"Rosamund!" There was terror in his voice now more than reproof. "Do—*please*—tell me what's going on? I went down to Mother's last night after I left the office— I knew she and Lindy had been seeing quite a lot of each other lately, and I wondered if perhaps Lindy'd mentioned anything—told her of some plan or other. Anyway, it seemed worth trying. So I went. And you know what Mother says?"—he gazed intently, desperately into Rosamund's face, as if he was seeking comfort rather than launching an accusation—"She says that you—you rang her up on Tuesday afternoon to say that Lindy wasn't coming after all, but that *you* were. Straight away, that same afternoon. You were just on the point of starting, you said——"

"*I* rang up?" The total incredulity in Rosamund's voice must have been convincing, for a flash of hope came into Geoffrey's face. It was clear that he desperately wanted to be convinced that his suspicions—whatever they were—were unfounded. He leaned forward eagerly— almost beseechingly, as if pleading with her to succeed in convincing him, by whatever means.

"*Didn't* you, then? Wasn't it you?"

"It most certainly wasn't!" declared Rosamund. "I'm surprised at Mother! She doesn't usually muddle telephone messages like that! Besides, she should know my voice by now, after nearly twenty years!"

"So you didn't ring at all? Not about next Sunday, or something like that? Something she could have misheard——?"

It was as if Geoffrey was frantically offering her all the let-outs he could think of—begging, praying her to make use of one or other of them. But Rosamund could only tell the truth as she saw it.

"No. I didn't ring her. There was nothing to ring about. But surely she must have realised, when I didn't turn up— Or do you mean that Lindy—?"

"No. No, that's the point. Neither of you turned up." For a second Geoffrey was grave again, then seemed forcibly to recover his precarious optimism. "Mother didn't really worry, of course, she took for granted it must have been the fog again. But she did think someone might have rung and told her."

"And my impersonator didn't bother, eh?" enquired Rosamund flippantly. "Well, I think they might have, after having created all the fuss!"

For a moment her flippancy jarred on both of them. The situation was too serious for this. Then, with one accord they seized on the flippancy, grasped it in both hands, as a lifeline in these unfathomable waters, in which both equally were slipping out of their depth.

"No manners, that's the trouble with your impersonator," grinned Geoffrey: and: "I'll demand references next time!" responded Rosamund, and the terrible moment was over.

No reason, really, why it should be. Nothing had been solved, explained, vindicated. It was all as mysterious as ever. But they had both simultaneously decided "let it be all right", and so it was all right. Such was their united strength, even now.

After breakfast, after Peter and Geoffrey had left the house, Rosamund sat down again in the kitchen, elbows on the table, chin in hand, and stared out across the toast crumbs, and the marmalade, and the bacon plates, into the strange new darkness that seemed to be encroaching on their lives.

For the mystery was growing. The fact that Geoffrey and she had succeeded this very morning in skipping away together from its advancing shadow did not mean that they would always be able to do this. The shadows would sweep towards them darker, faster, more relentless with every hour that Lindy did not return.

But it *must* be all right. Rosamund felt that she simply wasn't the kind of person who *could* do a thing like that, temperature or no temperature. That curious, vivid dream must have been sheer coincidence; and as for all the other clues, they were really too baffling to prove anything, one way or the other.

And now what about this story of her telephone call to her mother-in-law? How, if at all, could that be fitted into the bewildering, impossible picture?

Suppose—just suppose—that it was true. Suppose she really *had* set off for Ashdene that afternoon, instead of Lindy. Or as well as Lindy, perhaps. Suppose they had set off together, and had driven on and on, not to Ashdene at all, but on past it, through the towns, and the villages, and the council estates, nosing through the dripping winter lanes, flying over the glistening tarmac, on, on, swift as migrating swallows, over the great bare shoulders of the downs until they reached the sea?

Rosamund almost laughed as she sat alone in the untidy kitchen. For of course it hadn't happened. None of it had happened. Apart from all the other improbabilities, Lindy's car had been standing untouched outside Lindy's front gate during the whole of the upheaval, and was standing there still. Whatever had happened during that lost afternoon, it couldn't have involved going anywhere in Lindy's car.

Train, then? Suppose they had gone by train because of the fog? If the fog had been bad enough to prevent driving on Monday, then it would have prevented it on Tuesday too, it was still just as thick as ever. All right; so they had gone by train. They hadn't got off at Ashdene station, but had travelled on through the wintry country-side, stopping at every station, changing at Canterbury or somewhere, then on and on through——

Through fog, of course! The sudden illumination of this thought, the breathtaking release from fear, made Rosa-mund feel quite dizzy. Here at last was proof, final and complete, that her dream could have had no basis in real-ity. For where, on a damp, foggy December night, could there have been a wild wind blowing? How, in such weather, could she have seen stars, bright, big stars, wheeling in a black sky? And if these details of the dream were undoubted nonsense, then why give any credence to the rest? In a joyful resurgence of hope and confidence, Rosa-mund jumped up from her chair, cleared the table, and plunged zestfully into the washing up.

It was only when the downstairs work was finished, and she was about to go up and make the beds, that Rosamund felt uneasiness returning. For upstairs, in the bedroom, where her work was now about to take her, Lindy's battered bag still lay, unexplained, stuffed pell-mell out of sight into the wardrobe. And the muddy shoes, and the coat. These were not dreams. If she, Rosamund, had had no hand in Lindy's disappearance, then what on earth was going on? Still standing at the foot of the stairs, looking at them fearfully, like a bather confronted by ice-cold water, she tried to assemble some sort of theory that would explain all these extraordinary bits of in-criminating evidence.

It would have to be a fantastic theory, of course, that much was plain right from the start. Well, then: suppose someone was planning to murder Lindy, and wanted Rosamund to be accused of it? Before they embarked on the crime, they could have dressed up in Rosamund's shoes and coat so that the footprints and the bits of fluff and what not found near the body would be Rosamund's and not theirs. Then they could have put the bag in Rosamund's room for the police to practically fall over when they were called in; and then, to back up some complicated alibi, they must have put through a phone call to Mrs Fielding, imitating Rosamund's voice. *That* was a stumbling block. Mrs Fielding was no fool, she'd have known Rosamund's voice perfectly well.

But had it been Mrs Fielding herself who'd taken the call, or had it been Jessie? Rosamund tried to recall Geoffrey's exact words—*had* he implied, or definitely stated, that it was his mother, and not Jessie, to whom Rosamund was alleged to have spoken? But Jessie would have known her voice too. . . . Or was Jessie herself involved in the ever more tangled plot, perhaps innocently? All those relations of hers in Australia, for instance: there is something about relations in Australia which makes almost anything seem possible. Suppose Lindy had one of those millionaire uncles who are always dying in Australia and leaving their millions to unknown relatives on the other side of the world? And suppose the wicked nephew who would otherwise have inherited the money happened to be married to one of Jessie's nieces, and together they had come over to England to persuade Jessie that unless she pretended to have had a phone call from Rosamund, then her beloved mistress would be placed in terrible danger. . . .

By now it was clear even to its author that the story was getting out of hand. Perhaps, after all, the best thing to do would be to abandon all attempt at rational explanation: to succumb to the temptation of last night, and simply get rid of these nagging clues. They were after all doing no good; leading to nothing, solving nothing. Full of determination now, Rosamund set off upstairs, hurried into the bedroom over to the wardrobe.

The coat was just where she had left it; and so were the shoes; but the bag was gone.

Frantically she groped and grovelled in the dark interior flinging out shoes and garments pell-mell onto the floor. It *must* be here, she told herself, knowing already that it wasn't. It must have got pushed to the back. . . . Under this . . . behind that. . . .

It was fully five minutes before she gave up the pretence

of searching—five minutes whose real purpose was not to
find the handbag—for this, she knew, was already hopeless
—but to protect herself from facing too rapidly the alter-
native to finding it—the knowledge that Geoffrey must have
found it first.

Found it, and taken it away without a word.

CHAPTER XVIII

But Geoffrey would never behave in such a way! Before
the shock of her discovery had properly sunk in, Rosamund had already counteracted it by a thousand cer-
tainties concerning her husband's character. Geoffrey
was not a secretive man, nor even a reserved one. If he had
come across the bag in the wardrobe, he would instantly
have called out to Rosamund. "What on earth . . . ?" he
would have asked her . . . and how had it got here? . . . and
did she know about it . . . ? All his bewilderment would
have been laid immediately before her. He would never
have sneaked off with it like this, without telling her,
without offering her any chance of explaining.

But suppose he was afraid that she wouldn't be able
to explain—afraid, as he had been this morning about the
telephone call to Mother's? Might he not then, from sheer
horror, have avoided asking her, and instead have thought
up some explanation for himself—quickly, quickly, before
it had time to hurt, like dipping your finger in boiling water;
and then, driven by an ostrich-like impulse as powerful
as her own, he might simply have got rid of the bag. . . .

No. Even in fear for her, this wouldn't be like Geoffrey
. . . not the Geoffrey *she* knew, anyway. Someone else
must have taken it, then. Someone. . . . Anyone . . . and at
this point the whole puzzle spread out so vague, so vast,
that really it hardly seemed worth investigating at all.
Rosamund did not hope any longer to find an explanation.
The bag was gone, that was the main thing, and the only
thing she found herself hoping now was that it might be
gone for good. She did not want to have to think of it ever

again. Nor about any other of the clues. . . . Briskly she gathered up the shoes and coat, took them down to the garden, and proceeded swiftly and competently to brush away the mud. It was dry and brittle now, easy to remove. It tapped and pattered in little hard flakes onto the path, and soon it would be quite gone, merged for ever into the mud of a London garden. One more fall of rain, or even the heavy weight of dampness from one more winter's night, and the whole thing would never have happened, practically. She put away the well-polished shoes, hung up the clean, dry coat on its usual peg, and felt an absurd sense of achievement, as if by these trivial actions she had indeed reversed the course of time; made it flow backwards to the day before any of this had happened; ensured that Lindy should turn out never to have disappeared at all.

So vivid was this feeling that when the telephone rang she felt quite certain that she would hear Lindy's voice; and when she didn't, it took her quite a few seconds to recognise first whose voice it was, and then that the voice wasn't talking about the problem uppermost in her mind at all, but—as voices so often do—entirely about its own affairs.

"So could I possibly come, then, about five?" Norah's tiny voice was pleading, far away down the wires, while Rosamund was still trying to switch her thoughts into focus, away from her own problems and on to Norah's. "I'm so *desperately* worried about all this," the voice went on. "I *must* see you before William gets in."

"Oh course. Yes. Yes, I'd love to see you . . . yes, come as early as you like . . . no, of course I'm not too busy."

All the while she was reassuring Norah, Rosamund was trying to recollect what "all this" might refer to: Not the Lindy affair, of course. For Norah, "all this" must presumably refer to Ned—but what in particular had the boy been doing lately? Should she know?

Apparently she should. When Norah arrived that afternoon she seemed disconcerted—as well as a tiny bit offended—that Rosamund didn't seem to have heard the latest instalment of the Ned saga. But all hurt was swiftly obliterated by the pleasure and relief she evidently found in telling the story all over again, sitting forward in her

chair, and cradling her cup of tea between both hands in
nervous abstraction.

Ned had left home, it seemed—for about the sixth time,
to Rosamund's recollection—without consulting his parents, and since then they had had no news of him.

"Well, but he's done it before, hasn't he," Rosamund pointed out, in an attempt at consolation. "He never
seems to come to any harm. And as to writing, boys
never *do* write—they're all perfectly dreadful about letters. Really, I think you should stop worrying about it,
Norah; let him go his own way."

Futile advice, really; just as if Norah had any conceiv-
able means of *not* letting Ned go his own way. But nevertheless she seemed to derive some sort of comfort from
the suggestion, for her clutch on the cup of tea relaxed a
little, and she allowed herself to take a few spasmodic
sips.

"Yes, I know. I'm sure you're right, Rosamund, and I
try to feel like that—I *do* feel like that really. But this time
there's more to it than just him going away. I don't
know how to tell you really. . . ." She glanced nervously
around the room, as if in fear of hidden microphones, then
dropped her voice a little. "You see, the dreadful thing
is, when he went this time, I found he'd taken eight
pounds out of my bag! I don't know *what* would happen
if William were to find out. . . ."

"Oh, Norah! How dreadful for you!" Rosamund raked
her mind for words of comfort. "But can you be *sure*
he took it? . . . Couldn't you have lost it in some other
way?"

Norah shook her head.

"No. I just know it was there before lunch . . . and an
hour later it was gone, and he was gone! I discovered it
was missing *immediately*, you see; don't think that because I didn't tell you about it before, I didn't *know*
about it before. I knew about it the very day he went, but
I didn't like to tell you right there on the platform, it
seemed so public; and with your friend there, and everything. . . . I don't want people to know, you see, Rosamund.
I'm only telling you because I know you won't let it go
any further—I feel I can trust you. After all, you have a
son of your own, you can understand how I feel."

Rosamund did not quite like the implication that the

possession of Peter should necessarily make her familiar
with all the sensations of having money stolen from her
handbag; but poor Norah was in such distress, you couldn't
expect her to worry about being tactful. Besides, there
was something else in her little speech which Rosamund
really must take her up on, it was so puzzling.

"How do you mean, you didn't want to tell me 'right
there on the platform'? What platform? When do you
mean?"

Norah stared at her, bewilderment for a moment relaxing the anxious lines on her face.

"Why—on the station platform. Surely you remember?
When I was finding out about the trains to Brighton, the
very day Ned left. You *must* remember."

"But when was it? Which day?" Rosamund threshed
about in her mind for some recollection, but could find
none. "Which day?"

"Why, the day Ned left—I've just told you," Norah repeated, a little impatiently. "I knew already, while I was
talking to you both, that he'd taken the money, but as
I say, I didn't like———"

"Yes, yes, I know!" interrupted Rosamund desperately.
"But *when* was it? This week. . . . Last week . . . ?"

"Oh, do you feel like that too?" exclaimed Norah, in
tones of relief, as if she had at last found a fellow-suf-
ferer. "It's incredible, isn't it to realise that it's only
three days since he left! It seems like months and months.
. . . I'm *still* afraid he's gone to Brighton, you know. I
can't get it out of my mind."

"But what's so awful about Brighton?" Rosamund
allowed herself to be deflected for a moment. "Why
shouldn't he have gone to Brighton?"

"Oh, well. *You* know. Purple Hearts. Drink. That sort
of thing. And all those sort of girls———" Norah explained
delicately. "Isn't it Brighton where all that's supposed
to go on?"

"I should think it might go on anywhere," remarked
Rosamund. "I'd be surprised if Brighton was any worse
than London. If depends what set you get in with———"

"Yes, but that's the whole point!" Norah broke in desperately. "He *does* know a set in Brighton—I know he
does! That's why I was so anxious to find out if the booking office man remembered him buying a ticket. . . . I'm

so afraid that if he goes there he'll get into bad company!"

It occurred to Rosamund that if Ned had really stolen eight pounds from his mother's handbag, then it was the set in Brighton who were in danger of getting into bad company; but you could hardly say this to Ned's mother. Besides, she wanted to get the conversation back to the question that was puzzling her.

"So it was on Tuesday that you met me at the station?" she hazarded. "Was I catching a train, or something?"

She realised too late how idiotic the question must sound; but the blessed self-absorption of human beings in trouble saved her from looking foolish.

"Catching a train?" Norah repeated vaguely. "I don't know—I wasn't thinking about *catching* trains. I'd no intention of following Ned to Brighton, even if he *is* there. I think that would be most unwise, don't you? To make him feel pursued—persecuted? They do say, don't they," she continued, with the painstaking pride of one who has come rather late to this sort of thing, "that when a boy steals, it's *love* that he's really stealing; not money at all."

Rosamund could not help feeling that in Ned's case it was more likely to be money, especially if he intended living it up in Brighton without having to work; but she did not say so, since Norah seemed to be deriving some sort of comfort from the hypothesis.

"You may find," she suggested instead, "that he really feels he's only *borrowed* the money, and means to pay it back later. That wouldn't be stealing, would it, not in the ordinary sense."

For a minute Norah's face brightened.

"That's right! It wouldn't, would it! And even if, in the end, he didn't actually manage to pay me back, it still wouldn't have been *meant* as stealing, at the time. . . ." You could see Norah, like a little blind frantic mole, desperately flinging up her defences in advance against absolutely anything that might happen. She was well-insulated now, against the probability that Ned would never pay back the money.

Or was she? To her dismay, Rosamund noticed that while Norah still sipped at her cooling tea with grim intensity, tears were quietly welling into her eyes. She had never known Norah to cry before; like many anxious,

timorous people, always talking about their troubles,
Norah was yet deeply reticent about her real feelings.

"Oh, Norah, don't, I'm *sure* it'll be all right!" cried
Rosamund, distressed. "Really I'm sure! Ned's a good
boy at heart, I'm certain he is . . . this is all just a phase . . .
lots of boys go through it. . . . He'll come back!"

She poured forth, in sincere attempt at consolation, all
the optimistic platitudes that she always despised Norah
herself for expressing: but now Norah seemed to find no
solace in them.

"Oh, he'll come back all right!" she agreed bitterly.
"You needn't tell me *that!* But don't you understand—
that's the whole thing! I'm not really frightened of what
he'll do in Brighton—not the purple hearts, nor the
girls, nor the driving about in borrowed cars—none of it.
I've reached the point when I don't even *care!* All I'm
frightened of now is that in three days he'll be back—
right there in the house again, still bored, still with nothing he wants to do. . . . He'll lounge about the place again,
all day long, asking for money, being rude to his father,
making us quarrel about him all the time. . . . William and
I can never be happy again, never! That boy's round our
necks like a load of lead, we're chained to him for the
rest of our lives, it's a life-sentence! He'll never go away,
I know he won't, he'll never find anything he wants to do.
He'll stay at home making us miserable for the rest of
our lives. . . . And then they talk about *parents* being possessive! Oh, it's hopeless . . . hopeless. . . ."

Norah relapsed at last into unrestrained weeping, setting her cup blindly on the floor the better to concentrate.
"He's probably back home already!" she gulped, muffled
behind the huge handkerchief. "If you knew how I dread
the sight of that suitcase in the hall, and the rucksack, and
the tape recorder—he always takes every blessed thing,
as if he'd gone for ever, and every time there they all are
back again before the week is out. . . . And William in a
rage again, just when we'd been getting on a bit better
. . . and all that washing to do . . . and never being able to
get breakfast cleared away . . . !"

A sharp ring at the front door brought Norah's plaints
to a panic-stricken standstill. She jerked her tear-stained
face out of the handkerchief, and stared at Rosamund
in horror.

"It *can't* be six o'clock, can it?" she gasped, in a sort of cracked whisper.

"Yes. Just about." Rosamund glanced at the clock on the mantelpiece as she got up. "Don't worry, Norah; I won't bring them in here, whoever it is. . . ."

"But it'll be *William!*" protested Norah, in the same stricken whisper. "He's calling for me at six. . . . I'd no idea . . . it seemed like only a few minutes . . . !"

"Oh. Well——"

The bell rang again, more urgently. With her mind a blank as to what course of action she had best follow, Rosamund answered it, and sure enough it was William, morose and gloomy as ever.

"Norah ready?" he asked briefly, and stepped into the hall, naturally assuming that he was to be invited in. And indeed there was nothing else that Rosamund could do, in spite of knowing that Norah was cowering there in horror. And perhaps, after all, it would do William no harm to find his wife in tears for once, instead of eternally looking on the bright side. The bright side is all very well, but you don't want to absolutely rub a man's nose in it.

So Rosamund led William—as slowly as she could, for Norah's sake—through the hall, and when further delay was impossible, she flung open the sitting room door to reveal to him his weeping wife.

"Oh, hullo, William. You're just on time."

To Rosamund's astonishment—almost to her horror—all traces of tears had left Norah's cheeks. Her bright, tight little smile was in place as usual, and her red-rimmed eyes had been hidden by the hasty donning of a pair of reading glasses, which she so flashed about by little nervous movements of her head that they kept catching the light, and preventing any observer having a sustained view of the tell-tale eyes behind them.

"I'll come right away, William," she continued, getting up in nervous haste, stooping for her handkerchief . . . pretending to look for something on the mantelpiece . . . anything to keep her face averted.

William watched her grimly.

"That boy written yet?" he enquired brusquely, standing just inside the door. Norah looked away from him . . . plunged after her gloves.

"No—not just this afternoon," she replied brightly, for all the world as if they had been getting an affectionate letter by every post until this one. "But I'm sure we'll hear tomorrow. . . . I expect he's tried to phone, you know, several times, but of course I've been out rather a lot . . ."

"You must be crazy," commented her husband briefly. "Do you really believe that that boy'd waste one and twopence of his precious cash on setting his parents' minds at rest? Where's he got the money from, anyway, for this lark?" he enquired sharply. "I thought he hadn't a bean left?"

"Oh, well, you know, Ned is *very* frugal!" gabbled Norah, the smile growing brighter with every word until it quite distorted her small, gentle mouth. "I expect he's living rough, you know . . . economising . . . just until he·gets a job. I expect that's why he went off so suddenly, because he'd heard of some job. . . ."

"I'll bet it was!" said William grimly. "Some job around *here*, I'd say, that he's scared someone might make him take! Oh, yes, you're dead right, Norah; hearing of a job is enough to get *that* lad on the run, I don't doubt it!"

"Oh, but William, that's not fair!" wailed Norah. "I'm sure Ned wants to work really! It's just it's so difficult around here to get the right kind of job. That's why he's gone to try somewhere else, of course . . . the wisest thing, really. . . ."

Suddenly Rosamund couldn't bear the agony of that bright smile any longer, nor the thunderous misery that was growing minute by minute in William's face. Reckless of consequences, she broke in:

"Norah's terribly worried about Ned really," she said to William, clearly and firmly. "She's afraid that he'll never get a job—never achieve anything—never stand on his own feet. She's been crying her heart out about it for over an hour—right up till the very moment you came in. Take those glasses off, Norah. Let him see."

For a moment she thought her treachery would never be forgiven. The embattled pair stood for a moment staring at her as if she had hit them.

Then William took three strides across the room and whipped the glasses off his wife's face.

"Good God!" he said, staring at her red-rimmed eyes,

her blotchy cheeks. "Norah—you *are* worried? You really are."

He spoke wonderingly, like a man who has seen a new vision of hope. Then, with unwonted gentleness, he carefully gathered up his wife's scattered possessions for her and took her by the elbow.

"C'mon then. Mustn't be late, that won't help anything," he said gruffly, and steered her across the room; but from where she stood Rosamund could see that the expression of wonder was still in his eyes as he looked down at the little anxious woman on his arm: as if a worried, tearful, haggard wife was some priceless blessing that he had never thought to win.

"Don't you worry, old girl," Rosamund heard him say awkwardly, as the two passed through the little iron gate into the darkness. "The lad'll come out of it all right in the end. He'll work through it, you wait and see!"

And in his voice, even from this distance, Rosamund could hear the note of incredulous joy as William discovered that at last, for once, *he* was having a chance to be the optimistic one, the comforter.

CHAPTER XIX

Scarcely were the Pursers out of sight beyond the first street lamp when the front gate clanged once more and Peter bounded up the steps, coatless as usual in the winter cold, and radiating unaccustomed energy.

"Hullo, Mummy," he greeted Rosamund cheerfully. "I just met the two old crows going down the road. Been croaking around *here* again?"

"If you mean did Mr and Mrs Purser call," Rosamund corrected him haughtily, "then the answer is yes. They did." Really she would have liked to follow this up straight away with the news of Ned's escapade, but she felt that for decency's sake she should radiate dignified reproof for another minute or two. "Old crows indeed! My mother

would have *killed* me if I'd referred to her friends like
that," she mused righteously.

But Peter was always so amiable about everything,
that was the trouble. It disarmed you completely. He
seemed to have no idea, even now, that he was being
snubbed.

"Well, thank God they're not staying to supper, anyway," he observed, flinging himself into an armchair.
"They just make you feel you want to turn on the gas
oven and put them out of their misery, don't they?"

Even this was disarming in a way: this serene and
confident allying of himself and Rosamund together in
this inhospitable ambition. "What's the latest news, anyway, from Misery Mansions?"

He threw out the question in the most offhand manner,
as if it was all far beneath his attention really; but Rosamund knew very well that he thoroughly enjoyed any
gossip about the neighbourhood that she saw fit to repeat
to him. This, too, was endearing, and there was nothing
she could do but relent.

"Oh, just the usual," she said lightly. "Take your feet
off the rug, Peter, there's a good boy; you're absolutely
grinding the mud into it—— It's the usual story. Ned's
left home again."

"Good for him!" said Peter vaguely, and almost mean-
inglessly. He didn't particularly like Ned—hardly knew
him really—and certainly did not know enough about his
affairs or state of mind to have been able to form any
real opinion as to the rights and wrongs of his leaving
home. "Good for him" was simply a piece of automatic
conformity to the convention that all the young should
side together against all the old—or should talk as if they
did, anyway: actual life is quite another matter, as
any sensible young person knows.

"William and Norah are very worried about it, naturally," continued Rosamund—a little primly, in answer to
that "good for him!" "They're scared he may have
gone to Brighton, and got mixed up with gangs of de-
linquents and drug addicts and things."

"Good for him!" repeated Peter, parrot-like; and
then, focussing his attention: "Gone to Brighton, has he?
Then I daresay he's mixed up with that murder on the

line. *That'll* be something to liven up the old crows, won't it?"

Peter spoke with a cheerful relish which would have been moderately inoffensive if his remark had been the irrelevant nonsense which he naturally imagined it to be. But something—she had not yet collected her wits enough to say what—flicked at Rosamund's ever-present uneasiness, and she pulled him up sharply.

"What murder?"

Peter looked a little surprised.

"What? Oh, I don't know. Not really. Just there's supposed to have been a murder—well, a body found, anyway —near a bit of the Southern railway. Not Brighton particularly, I only said that to make it more interesting, since Ned's gone there. No, it was on the Ashdene line actually, somewhere on the way to Granny's. Though now I come to think of it, you *can* get to Brighton that way. If you change about twenty times. . . ."

"Who told you? How do you know?"

Rosamund tried to keep the tension out of her voice. Somehow, she had to fit this jig-saw puzzle together without letting her anxiety show. Thank goodness for the self-absorption of the young—well, of everybody, really. . . .

"Well, look it up in the timetable for yourself—— Oh, you mean about the murder? I heard about it at school."

"But *who*? Who actually told you——?"

"Some chaps at school," repeated Peter amiably, apparently not bothering to wonder why his mother was suddenly displaying such an uncharacteristic interest in this isolated bit of news. "There was a lot of talk about it yesterday, because two of the chaps said they'd actually *seen* the body. A woman. Lying on the bank beside the line."

"But how could they know she was dead?" Rosamund wished she could stop asking questions, but she couldn't. Peter looked at her pityingly.

"Well, she wouldn't be sunbathing, would she, in the pitch dark, on a December evening? Anyway, they just *did* know. They'd gone right up to her, so 'tis said. Tried to wake her. She's popped it all right. When's supper?"

"Quite soon. *Who* did you say found her? Two of your friends?"

"Nope. Fourth-formers. But why ever do you want to know all this, Mummy?"—Peter was at last stirred to mild protest—"You don't *really* think I meant all that about Ned Purser, do you? I was only fooling——!"

"Of course! I know you were, dear!" Rosamund assured him hastily. "It's just—well, I'm just interested, that's all. Anybody might be—and since it was on the way to Granny's naturally it makes it that bit more interesting. Is it in the papers yet, do you know? Murders usually are."

"Don't think so. Haven't seen anything. Anyway, it only happened two or three days ago. It might be in the local paper, I suppose, at the weekend. Perhaps in Granny's, you'd better ask her. Or Jessie. I expect she keeps up with the murders better than Granny does."

Impossible to go on with the inquisition any longer. Peter was already mildly puzzled by her insistence, and would become disastrously so if she kept hammering on any longer. Anyway, she knew in her heart that there was nothing left to ask. All the pieces of the puzzle were now in her hands; all she needed was a few minutes of quiet and solitude to fit them together. Quiet so that she wouldn't become confused; solitude so that no one would be there to watch her face changing, as the picture took shape, from the face of a pleasant, ordinary housewife to the face of someone looking at a monstrosity.

Or had the change already come? What sort of face was it, even now, that smiled at Peter across the hearth; what sort of voice was it that was telling him to go up to his room and try to get some of his homework done before supper? It was strange, almost eerie, the way Peter didn't seem to notice any difference in her. Here he was, obeying with exactly the usual amount of grumbling and delay, for all the world as if it was his own mother speaking, not a murderess at all.

How had she let this word slip past her guard? As if it was a physical assailant, she fought it back, forced it from her mind, and then turned, like an animal at bay, to face the mighty weight of evidence massing against her from every side.

For it was no longer just the coincidence of her dream and Lindy's disappearance; no longer the puzzle of the handbag and the muddy shoes. Everything now was conspiring to show that she really *had* travelled down to Ashdene that Tuesday afternoon. As well as her alleged telephone call to her mother-in-law, there was now Norah's word for it that Rosamund and "your friend" had been seen on the station platform. Rosamund's annoyance at being unable to extract from Norah any further details, such as who her companion was, which platform they were on, and at exactly what time, was really a contrived annoyance. She had no doubt what the answers would be. The companion was Lindy: the platform, the one for Ashdene: the time, Tuesday afternoon.

And now the body by the line. . . . She recalled this morning's brief, false assurance that, because of the fog, her dream of wind and stars couldn't possibly fit the facts. She had taken comfort from the thought that on such a night there could be no wind blowing even on a cliff top, no stars to be seen. But there need be no cliffs in the picture now, nor any stars. That thunder of crashing seas could have been the thunder of a speeding train, the noise magnified to terror as the compartment door swung open, letting in the wild wind of speed to roar about her face, the myriad lights and sparks of the railway world to spin before her eyes as she gave that light push that was all that was needed . . . you would not need to use violence if you took your victim by surprise. . . .

Some dim and terrible memory thrust for one fraction of a second against the walls of her consciousness, then died away; it left her trembling, her head aching all over again, as if from a savage blow.

She felt numbed, stupefied. She scarcely noticed when Geoffrey came in; when Peter came down from doing his homework; when she dished up stew, and mashed potatoes, and apple pie for them both. Nor could she have said what they all talked about during the meal; yet it must have been something fairly ordinary, and she must have taken her usual part, for neither of them were asking her what was the matter, or looking at her in a puzzled way.

What were they both thinking? What did they think she was thinking, as she moved quietly about the kitchen, changing plates, setting food before them? Never had she felt so completely alone, as if during the past few hours she had travelled without noticing it to somewhere indescribably remote; had crossed some frontier into a land where no one else could follow.

But you couldn't go on feeling like that, not right through the washing up and everything. After she had put away the last of the glasses, and hung the towel back on its hook, Rosamund suddenly and surprisingly found herself in contact with Geoffrey again, in a manner strained and sad, but oddly close. As they moved out of the kitchen and towards the sitting room, Geoffrey turned towards her and began to say: "Well, I think I'll . . ." and stopped. "Have a look at the paper," he finished in a mumble; but they both knew what, from long habit, he had been going to say. "Pop over to Lindy's for a bit" were the words he had swallowed; and the desolation of it swept them both, simultaneously and without a word. The cheerless silence of the house next door seemed in that moment to spread into this house; the silence, the enigma, the sudden emptiness in both their lives.

Yes, in Rosamund's too; for as she looked into her husband's eyes she knew that the destroying of the Other Woman can bring no surcease of jealousy; rather the reverse, for where there is no longer any battle ground, there is no longer any hope of victory. The cobwebs gather in the arena now, and the dust thickens, and the dead wind blows out of the past bringing no hope nor glory; only the emptiness of a spirit that can fight no more.

Something of her sense of desolation Geoffrey must have seen in her face, for he gripped her hand in a quick gesture.

"Oh, Rosamund, you were so fond of her, too!" he exclaimed; and for a moment they stood in the kitchen doorway exchanging wordless comfort. *"Were* so fond of her"—for the first time, Geoffrey was speaking as if he felt in his heart that Lindy was dead.

Rosamund should have felt sick with guilt: she should have felt appalled at herself for accepting from her husband comfort so misdirected, so undeserved. Yet somehow she did not. The comfort seemed utterly appropriate; that moment of shared grief was something self-contained, like a crystal, invulnerable. It seemed to have nothing to do with what either of them had done, felt or not felt; nothing to do with crimes or virtues, not even with truth or lies. And even after it was all over, and Geoffrey was hidden unhappily behind the newspaper in the big armchair, it was still not guilt that swept through Rosamund's soul; rather it was a sense of futility so huge as to defy rational appraisal. How *could* I have done this thing, she asked herself, to no purpose and with no outcome? I must have seen then, just as I can see now, that the only possible result of Lindy's death, even from my own selfish point of view, must be this sense of emptiness and loss. Lindy's death doesn't restore Geoffrey to me; it simply leaves him emptier, poorer; from now on he will have less to give me, not more. Even if he never learns of my share in it, it will nevertheless remain as a great wall between us, shutting out the sun, preventing any further growth in our marriage. If Lindy had stayed alive, then his love—his fondness—for her might have died a thousand natural deaths; she might, as the months and years went by, have disillusioned him in a thousand different ways; I myself might have learned much from my own jealousy; we could all have emerged from it richer, wiser. But now his feeling for her will be preserved as in amber, for ever at its peak, for ever proof against the inroads of time, of boredom, of human changeability. . . .

No! I could never have been such a fool! Rosamund was almost startled at this conclusion to her musings. Not: I could never have been so wicked! or: I could never have been so cruel! Just: I could never have been such a fool.

I couldn't; no. But who is this "I" that is to be considered? If, during that strange, lost afternoon, I was delirious—mad—what you will—then was the "I" of those hours anything I could hope to recognise as myself? They say, don't they, that when the unconscious mind takes charge, then primitive instinct and passions come to the fore which the ordinary conscious, rational person would utterly repudiate?

And what are the conditions most likely to bring the unconscious mind to the fore like this? Surely "They" would all agree that months of suppression of jealousy; months of smiling to cover the black hatred in one's heart; months of biting back the bitter, censorious words, and forcing friendly speeches onto one's tongue. . . . Why, it is practically a case-history as it stands . . . !

For long, black minutes Rosamund's rising horror

struggled with what she still tried to call common-sense. Out of the past months, one episode after another arose, bright, black, and clear, like silhouettes against the uncomprehended blur of her conscience. The moments when she had hated Lindy most—and had forced herself to speak brightly and kindly. The moments when hopes of Lindy's death had been clear and vivid in her mind—and she had forced herself to smile. . . . All these repressions and deceptions, could they have risen in revolt at last . . . and then could her horrified consciousness, in its guilt and terror, have blacked out the memory of that culmination of her hatred?

"They" would say it could, undoubtedly. "They" would say that amnesia is invariably the mind's final refuge from intolerable guilt.

Suddenly Rosamund longed for some really silly person, like Carlotta perhaps, or Norah, to ring on the doorbell at this very moment, and come in and chatter to her about inhibitions and guilt-complexes and such: the kind of person who, in a few brief, earnest sentences, can make you *know* that psychology is all nonsense.

CHAPTER XX

But the person who did ring the doorbell, at about nine o'clock, was no amateur psychologist to chatter reassuring claptrap about hidden drives. On the contrary, it was Walker.

"He's upstairs doing his homework," said Rosamund at once, obligingly saving Walker the weariness of opening his mouth and asking for Peter: and silently, evasively, as if outwitting an enemy sentry, he darted past her and up the stairs to Peter's room. Peter's voice sounded for a moment; he seemed pleased and surprised; and then the door closed and the sound of voices was quenched.

It was too quiet, too deathlike, and Rosamund could not feel at ease anywhere in the whole house. Not in the

sitting room, where her husband's unhappy quietness
hovered round her like an accusation; nor in the bedroom
where it was too early to go to bed; nor in the kitchen
where the washing up was all finished and there was
nothing left to do.

Driven by the stillness, Rosamund began to contem-
plate going in next door, to the darkened house where
Lindy was no more. Perhaps, after all, it *wasn't* darkened now? Perhaps Eileen was home already? She'd
said she intended going straight after work this evening
to visit some elderly relative who just *might* have some
knowledge of Lindy's whereabouts, but she might have
changed her plans; the relative might have been out, or
away, or something. And at least, at the very worst, there
would be Shang Low there, barking disagreeably, breaking the doom-laden silence, demanding to be taken for
a walk. Even that would be better than nothing.

Yes, very much better. Decidely reassuring, in fact,
because you couldn't imagine a *murderess* taking a dog
for a walk . . . wandering slowly, peaceably along the
winter roads, bidding "good evening" to the neighbours
. . . pausing for a chat with this one . . . enquiries after the
health of that one . . . sharing a good-natured smile over
Shang Low's obstinacy as he dragged her towards this
lamppost or that. Besides, the neighbours wouldn't *be*
like that if she were a murderess. They would see it in her
face, even if they were not consciously aware of what they
saw . . . they would hurry on, with a single uneasy word,
if she stopped to greet them . . . they would glide past on
the other side of the road . . . they would whisper uneasily
together. . . . Yes, her walk with Shang Low would be a
test, it would *prove* that everything was all right.

In picturing this imaginary walk which was so smoothly
and effortlessly to prove her innocence, Rosamund was
beginning to forget that her original plan had been to call
on Eileen if she was in; so it was with quite a shock that
she saw, as she emerged from her own front gate, that
there was a light shining in Eileen's upstairs room.

Well, that was all right. That was what she had hoped
for in the first place. All she had to do now was to go up the
path and ring the bell.

Yet for some reason she was trembling, assailed by
an extraordinary sense of embarrassment, almost as if

she was wearing some sort of fancy dress. She felt, as she stood hesitating in the dark garden, as if she didn't belong here at all—had no right to go and ring that bell: just as you might feel if you were returning to the neighbourhood after long years away, wondering if people would still recognise you. . . .

And for one terrible second, it seemed that Eileen did not. Her blank, stricken face seemed to confirm every fear, fanciful or real, that had been seething in Rosamund's brain ever since this evening's revelations. But almost at once, Eileen's expression changed—or rather, Rosamund recognised it for what it was—simple disappointment.

"Oh! Oh, Rosamund. How nice." You could see Eileen adjusting herself to the new, unexciting situation. "Do come in, won't you?"

Her tone was not enthusiastic, but Rosamund nevertheless accepted the half-hearted invitation; and as soon as she had her visitor inside the front door, Eileen began to seem a little more welcoming. Having recovered from the first shock of disappointment, she was no doubt beginning to feel that Rosamund might be better than nothing as company.

"Come up to my room, will you?" she urged. "I've got the gas fire on. It doesn't seem worth while keeping the sitting room going when . . . that is . . ."

For one ridiculous second Rosamund felt Eileen's embarrassment as an accusation: as if Eileen was laying at *her* door the chilly desolation of the sitting room. But she knew really that such a notion was absurd. . . . She hastened to dispel the uncomfortable atmosphere engendered by Eileen's evasive phraseology and her own headlong interpretation of it.

"No, of course not. And its so cosy, isn't it, living in a bed-sitting-room, you don't have to turn out into a cold room to go to bed. Any news?"

There was no hypocrisy in Rosamund's eager question, even though she felt that she already knew—and intended to keep to herself—far more than Eileen could possibly have to tell her. Yet somehow she was still eager to hear Eileen's "news", just as a child may be eager to hear a bedtime story, however nonsensical, to sustain and comfort it through the long dark night.

"No. Not really. But somehow, tonight, I *do* feel a little bit more hopeful," said Eileen surprisingly, settling her visitor in the only armchair in the small bedroom, and turning the gently-hissing gas fire as high as it would go. "I found that Auntie Min was away, you see, and so —— Would you like some cocoa, or something?" she interrupted herself awkwardly, a little ungraciously, as she recollected her duties as hostess—usually so capably taken over by Lindy. You could hear in her voice what a nuisance it would be to have to stop the story before it began, and go down to the kitchen and mess about with saucepans and jugs. Rosamund thought it would be a nuisance too, so she hastily declined, and Eileen, greatly relieved, continued: "and anyway, I didn't really think Auntie Min could know much, we haven't seen her for ages. But as I came away—as I was waiting for a bus—it suddenly occurred to me that there is one possibility that none of us have mentioned. The more I think about it the more likely I think it is, it cheers me up no end. Though perhaps—I don't know—perhaps I shouldn't expect it to cheer *you* up? Perhaps I shouldn't tell you—I don't want you to be upset. . . ."

She laughed, an embarrassed little sound, and looked at Rosamund enquiringly. Rosamund felt irritated. When people embarked on this sort of apologetic preamble it was never really to save you being hurt: it was just to save them from feeling responsible for it.

"Well—go on. Tell me!" said Rosamund rather sharply. "After all, nothing could be worse than. . . ." But of course Eileen didn't know yet *what* it couldn't be worse than.

"Yes! Of course! I hoped you'd take it like that!" exclaimed Eileen in over-hasty relief. "It's just that—well, you know Lindy was—is—very fond of your husband, don't you?"

"Well, it did cross my mind," said Rosamund drily. "And so?"

"Oh, not in any *bad* way," Eileen rattled on, flustered. "I mean, she wouldn't dream of breaking up a happy marriage, nothing like that. . . ."

"She wouldn't?" Rosamund simply couldn't help it. The sarcastic little phrases slipped from her throat as involuntarily as hiccups. Eileen raced on: "So I wondered—you see, I've known about the way she felt for some

time—I couldn't help it, being so close to her—but I didn't
know if *you* knew, or even if your husband did. Lindy
hides her feelings so *very* well, doesn't she? And I wasn't
even sure if she was right about the way she thought
he felt—I mean, he's such a kind man, isn't he, I thought
sometimes that perhaps Lindy was mistaking his kindness
for. . . . Well, anyway, that's why, when he asked me that
night if I knew any reason why Lindy should be—worried—I didn't know what to say. I didn't like to tell
him, in case he didn't know, but of course she *was* worried, she must have been, about the way *she* felt, and
about not knowing how *he* felt. . . . And then, when he
said she'd sounded *scared* . . . it quite frightened me
when he said it. . . . I began imagining all sorts of things
. . ." she glanced at Rosamund quickly and uneasily, then
went on: "But now I begin to feel that it may all be much
simpler than we think. It may be simply that Lindy felt
that the situation was getting—well, she may have felt
that the only way to prevent it going too far was simply
for her to disappear. Just as she has done, without telling
anyone, without leaving an address or anything—to give
herself a chance to sort out her own feelings? Something
like that?"

Eileen's eyes looked wide and childlike, full of uncertainty and hope. Confronted by all this youth and naïvety,
Rosamund suddenly felt herself very old and powerful;
the possessor of all kinds of secret knowledge, whereas
Eileen was merely the poor little dupe. For all these reasons she must be very gentle in disillusioning Eileen.
Yet even as she opened her mouth to speak, she knew
she couldn't be gentle.

"I think Lindy's feelings were perfectly sorted out all
along," she said levelly. "She knew exactly what she
wanted. And how to get it."

Eileen sensed the hostility at last.

"Oh, you're not being *fair* to Lindy!" she cried. "No
one is! People think she's just man-mad—a husband
snatcher—that sort of thing. But she *isn't*. She's just the
opposite really!"

Rosamund recalled Basil's hints to this effect the other
night. Her bitterness was replaced for a moment by curiosity.

"How do you mean?" she asked, as she had asked

Basil. "Do you mean it's all put on, this *femme fatale* act?"

"Oh, not *put on!*" protested Eileen, bristling up defensively on her sister's behalf. "It's more that she's honestly worked on herself over the last few years—tried to make herself more attractive—and what's wrong with that, anyway?" She turned on Rosamund belligerently, although Rosamund had said nothing. "It's what all women do, in one way or another!"

"Well, of course," agreed Rosamund mildly. "Naturally. We all do. It's just that—with Lindy—she seems to devote herself to it so—so sort of non-stop. And it seems rather surprising that she should *need* to go to all that trouble. I'd have thought she was attractive enough anyway."

"Oh—well, yes, of course she is," said Eileen hastily. "But you see, you never knew her the way she *used* to be. You'd understand better if you had. You should have known her—seen her—as she was five years ago. Believe it or not, she seemed quite middle-aged then, she really did. Even I noticed it, and so did my school friends, they used to treat her exactly as if she was one of the mothers. She was terribly shy, I realise now, and never went out anywhere, or had any boy friends; she had no idea how to dress—and I never remember seeing her wearing make-up, or with her hair done any fancy way—nothing. But of course, I realise now, it wasn't her fault; she'd never had a chance. She'd had me to bring up, you see, ever since our parents died . . . it made her get into the way of acting middle-aged—being a housewife, you know— before she'd ever had the chance to be young! Can't you understand?"

"Yes, of course."

Rosamund was speaking mechanically. Understanding formed no part of her thoughts at this moment. All she could feel was a rising and totally unexpected fury at this new light on Lindy's character. Just like Lindy! she found herself thinking furiously: she has not only stolen my husband's affection, but now she has got to be pitied for it as well! I've got to feel *sorry*, now, for this poor, shy, plain creature who had to struggle so hard to make herself attractive enough to destroy my marriage! I've got to admire her pluck—understand the struggle she's been through! Well, I won't, I just won't, I don't *want* to understand her, ever; and if I haven't murdered her already, then I damn well *will*, the very next time I lay eyes on her! And there'll be nothing subconscious about it, either: I mean to enjoy it *this* time!

Were these the sort of thoughts that would go through the mind of a *real* murderess? Surely not! All the same, Rosamund was dismayed by the violence of her own emotions—disproportionate, surely, to the immediate provocation? She tried to analyse them as best she could, and discovered that part at least of the motive force behind them consisted of a ridiculous feeling that Lindy had deliberately suffered a frustrated girlhood in order to make it wickeder than ever of Rosamund to have murdered her. The absurdity of this train of feeling—you could hardly call it thought—sobered her; she strove to recover some sort of equanimity. Natural curiosity came to her aid.

"What made her suddenly change?" she asked.

"Oh, but don't you see? As soon as *I* was off her hands, as soon as she didn't have to feel responsible for me any more—why, then she at last had the chance to be young! But by then she was past thirty, and of course, at that age, being young is something that has to be *learnt,* it doesn't just happen any more. It made me so happy to watch her beginning to experiment with her hair; with different sorts of lipstick; learning to be amusing, witty, and to talk about the sort of things that interest men. Oh, I understood just how it was for her—but no one else ever did, not even Basil——*Oh!*"

Eileen broke off in mid-sentence, and the look in her eyes as the door swung open made you feel that she was already leaping up; rushing across the room with arms outstretched. It was quite a shock to find that she wasn't; that she was still sitting on the divan, neat and tense.

"Hullo, Basil," she said in a tiny voice, making no move towards him. He, too, made no move; just stood in the doorway, looking at her; and Rosamund wondered if he was aware of his power. She wondered, too, what should be *her* rôle in the situation. Should she just get up and go straight away, and leave them alone together?

"Nice to find you here, Mrs Fielding!" said Basil gallantly; and, "Don't go, Rosamund, please!" murmured Eileen, with apparent sincerity. Rosamund hesitated. It occurred to her that perhaps her presence really was a relief to them both; a sort of buffer against the first impact of an encounter which, deliberately sought though it may have been, was bound at first to bring as much embarrassment as pleasure to both of them.

"I'm glad Eileen's found a bit of company," continued Basil coming properly into the room. "Do tell me what you were talking about—it sounded fascinating. Something about me!" He looked eagerly from one to the other, like a conceited little boy, and Rosamund could hardly help laughing.

"We were saying . . . Eileen was saying . . . that we none of us understand Lindy properly, and——"

"I didn't! We weren't!" Eileen seemed so flustered in her denials that Rosamund wondered what she had said amiss. "I was only saying"—Eileen painstakingly shifted the emphasis—"that perhaps we needn't worry too much about Lindy—about her disappearing, I mean. I was just telling Rosamund that I believe she may have run away because she's found that she's in love with Rosamund's husband——"

"Oh, rubbish!" All Basil's embarrassment seemed to have left him, and he settled himself astride a little cane chair, arms folded along its back, apparently highly content to reassume his husbandly prerogative of contradicting everything Eileen said. "Lindy's never been in love with anybody, and never will be; and I'm quite sure Mrs Fielding's husband isn't in love with *her*! You didn't really think he was, did you?" He turned towards Rosamund.

"Well—I——"

"I daresay he *likes* her well enough," continued Basil with an assumption of omniscience which in this case seemed endearing rather than irritating. "Most men do. Naturally they like being flattered and made much of— who doesn't? But she's not the least bit attractive to them, not really. And she knows it. That's why she goes in for all this flattery and good-time-ery—it's a substitute. As I told you before, this gaiety-girl business is all fairly new. It's not natural to her. She's one of Nature's frumps, really. I told you."

"Oh, Basil, she's *not*! It's just that while she had me to look after, she never had the chance——"

"Oh, come off it, Eileen! There's no such thing as 'not having the chance'! A girl who'd got what it takes wouldn't have been put off by having a kid sister in tow! Use your sense. Lindy *hadn't* got what it takes—still hasn't, though I must hand it to her that she's learnt to put up a pretty dazzling façade. But it annoys me, Eileen, that it should take *you* in. You seem to lose all your sense of humour where Lindy's concerned, you turn into a horrid little prig! That's really what I've always had against her, you know. I never really minded old Lindy doing her stuff —all those ridiculous parties and candles and whatnot. Good luck to her, I thought, if she wants to play it that way. But when it came to never being allowed to laugh at her, or to say anything at all that might prick holes in her fancy picture of herself . . . and then having to stand by and listen to her talking as if *you* were the frumpish one—as she did, Eileen, in the end, you know she did— and you taking it lying down. . . ."

"I didn't! That is, I should hope I did!" Eileen stumbled momentarily amid her conflicting denials, then went gamely on: "I tried to, anyway, because I knew very well that she didn't really mean it. She was only trying to give herself confidence. . . . And that's all she's doing now, really, in making Geoffrey fall in love with her. That's why it's so desperately important to her—the most important thing that's ever happened in her life. She just wants to know for certain that she *can* make a man fall in love with her—that she can fall in love herself. She *needs* to know——"

"Well, how do you like that, Mrs Fielding? Having your husband prescribed for Lindy as if he was a bottle of medicine on the Health Service? But I wouldn't worry. As I say, I *know* he isn't in love with her——"

"And I say he is!" Eileen defied him. "Apart from anything else, it's well known that men always fall in love with the same sort of women over and over again. And Rosamund and Lindy are *terribly* alike!"

"*Me*?" Rosamund was too much astounded for resentment. "How on earth——?"

"Well——" Eileen studied her with careful honesty. "Not in looks so much, perhaps—but—— Well, you're both terribly proud, for one thing; you'd do anything rather than admit to any sort of weakness. And you both have the same

sort of odd, witty, spiteful sort of thoughts that you suddenly come out with—or not, as the case may be—one
can never tell what you're really thinking, either of you.
You're both born schemers: and you'd both rather die
than not appear to advantage. . . . You see, I'm not blind
to Lindy's faults!"—she was talking to Basil now, not to
Rosamund, evidently seizing the opportunity for capping
a long-standing argument. "You see, I *don't* always see
Lindy through rose-coloured spectacles——!"

Basil's face softened. With a quick, unrehearsed gesture,
he leaned across the little space between them and took
Eileen's hand.

"Oh, Eileen, why do you have to say that—just when
I was beginning to think that it must be your rose-coloured
spectacles that I love you for! At least, I would if they
were turned on *me* a little bit more often! And I love you
for your loyalty, too, I always have, it's just that it's so
damned irritating as well. . . ."

Rosamund judged that now it really *was* time for her
to disappear. All embarrassment between the re-united
couple—if re-united they should finally prove to be—had
been washed away in disputation—evidently a familiar
medium to them both.

And as Rosamund slowly re-entered her own unnaturally quiet home, she could hardly have said which thought
was now disturbing her most—the thought that she might
prove to be a murderess, or the thought that Eileen was
perhaps right, and she really was "terribly like Lindy".

CHAPTER XXI

"Oh, by the way, Mummy," called Peter from the front
steps, just as he was leaving for school next morning:
"They rang up from Ashdene last night. They want you
to go down."

Rosamund hurried from the kitchen, wiping her hands
on a tea-towel. She caught him at the gate.

"What for? When? You might have told me, Peter!"

"Well, I *am* telling you," Peter pointed out, manoeuvring his bicycle through the gate, impatient to be gone.

"Wait, Peter, do tell me a bit more about it. What did Granny say, exactly? Has anything happened?"

"*I* don't know," said Peter, one foot on the pedal already. "It was Walker answered the phone, not me. From what he says, I don't think it could have been Granny, it must have been Jessie or someone, but anyway, they want you to come down as soon as you can manage it. They sounded in a bit of a flap, Walker says, but I wouldn't worry, Mummy, not really. You know how Walker always exaggerates everything."

For a moment Rosamund was distracted from the main issue as she made (not for the first time) a dazed sort of effort to relate the Walker she knew to the one that Peter appeared to know; but as always, it was useless. Meanwhile Peter and his bicycle, like a single organism, had sailed off into the stream of morning traffic, and she was left to ponder this new development as best she could.

She must go down to Ashdene, of course, by the earliest train possible, and see what it was all about. Her mind began to seethe, not with anxieties but with trivial plans. The expedition might take all day, so she must leave something ready for Geoffrey's and Peter's supper, and a note explaining where she had gone. A note for the laundry man too, and for the window cleaner, and for the man who had failed to come and look at the boiler for the last six weeks, but who would undoubtedly come today. Oh, and she must tell Eileen that she couldn't after all look in and feed Shang Low, she must find someone else: with luck, Eileen wouldn't have left for work yet.

But she had. It was Basil who opened the door, in a maroon silk dressing gown and looking very pleased with himself, very much master of the establishment. He listened carefully to Rosamund's problem, ignored the Shang Low aspect of it, but offered at once to drive her down to Ashdene.

"I've got to meet a chap in Rochester," he explained. "So it'll be right on my way, and I don't mind getting there a bit early—give me a chance to spy out the land a bit before I have to commit myself."

Rosamund still didn't know what Basil's job was—she

had never remembered to ask him at any of the appropriate moments. Perhaps she had heard right originally, and he *was* a Shell Shelder, and perhaps Shell Shelders do have to meet chaps in Rochester for lunch, why not? Anyway, this didn't seem the moment to find out, so while he went off to get dressed, she once more enlisted the help of the obliging Dawsons for Shang Low's daily routine.

By ten o'clock they were on their way in Basil's small, spitting car, about which he talked the whole time. He was still young enough to feel it was a status symbol to have bought the vehicle for only five pounds; and while he described with self-absorbed gusto all the things that had been wrong with it and that he had managed to put right, Rosamund was able to devote her thoughts almost entirely to her own problems. In all the bustle and arrangements of this morning she had almost forgotten that she might be a murderess; and now, speeding through the familiar countryside, the whole idea seemed more than ever ridiculous. While Basil's voice went soothingly on about the gear-changes or something, she set herself yet again to review her situation.

For one brief, unpleasant second the weight, the immensity of the evidence piling up against her filled her with a sick terror, quite out of keeping with the bright morning . . . then, almost at once, she found herself able to treat its very immensity as a challenge, a positive stimulus to her powers of repudiation. To be able to defy effectively such a mountainous array of undisputed fact seemed to her this morning like a sign of returning health, a successful convalescence of the spirit. As if the acceptance of undeniable facts was a sort of illness from which she was recovering rapidly, thank you very much, in this bright winter sunshine. The sight of her grey skirt, her smart black shoes, helped her a lot in her solitary battle against the evidence. Murderesses just *don't* dress like that; and they don't worry about leaving cold suppers ready for their husbands and sons, either; nor about the laundry, nor about feeding the neighbours' dogs. . . . It was all so madly out of character, Rosamund told herself, that there *must* be some other explanation. Even the story about the millionaire uncle in Australia seemed more plausible . . . though of course Norah would have to be fitted into it now, as well as all the others; and the fourth form chaps from Peter's school, too, who said they'd seen a body by the line. All these people, all bent on incriminating Rosamund by means of these elaborate lies! The fourth form chaps, of course, could have been bribed by a secret agent, or persuaded that they were doing a patriotic service by pretending to have seen a body: but what about Norah? She seemed a sadly un-ruthless character to get mixed up in such an affair; and a muddle-headed one, too; she'd tell all the wrong lies to the wrong people. Perhaps she had, of course; perhaps Rosamund wasn't the person she'd been supposed to lie to at all? Oh, but wait: supposing it was *Ned* who was heir to the Australian millions, not the wicked nephew who'd married Jessie's niece at all? But in that case, where did Jessie's niece come into it? By now, the author had quite forgotten by what process of reasoning Jessie's niece had been cast in her unhappy role; and anyway, Basil was now saying "isn't it?" for the second time, so the least she could do was start attending to him for a little.

It was the noises made by his little car to which he was drawing Rosamund's attention, lots and lots of rare and wonderful noises, every one of which meant something to him, though to Rosamund they all sounded the same. He looked utterly happy and self-absorbed, like a mother displaying a baby who is just learning to talk, bedazzled by the unrealistic assumption that other people, too, will regard this as speech.

They had left home in bright winter sunshine, but by the time Basil dropped Rosamund outside her mother-in-law's house, there was no doubt that the fog was coming back. The sun was still shining, but there was a haze over it: soon it would be a mere silvery disk in the gathering greyness, and after that it would be gone.

Rosamund shivered. The air was damp, and growing colder. She hurried up the short gravel drive, past the winter evergreens, and rang thankfully on the familiar old door, heard Jessie's familiar steps crossing the hall, unhurried but without delay.

"Oh, Miss Rosamund! It's good to see you!" The old servant's pleasure was even more marked than usual, and Rosamund responded warmly.

"It's good to see you, Jessie, too," she said. "How are you keeping?"

"Pretty fair, thank you Miss Rosamund," replied Jessie, as she always did. "And you, Miss . . ." she stopped, examined Rosamund's face more closely. "You don't look too good, Miss Rosamund, you don't look too good at all. Haven't you been quite the thing lately?"

Rosamund felt oddly put out by Jessie's concern. No woman *likes* to be told that she doesn't look well, of course; but Rosamund, for some reason, found the comment not merely unflattering, but somehow unnerving. It gave her an inexplicable little shock of fear . . . spoilt the familiar peace and enjoyment of arriving here.

"Oh, I'm all right, Jessie, thank you," she brushed it aside quickly. "I had a touch of 'flu, you know, at the beginning of the week, but I'm all right now."

"Oh, the 'flu, was it, Miss Rosamund?" Jessie seemed, for some reason, greatly relieved. "So *that* was why you never come when you rung, last Tuesday. We was wondering, just a little, Mrs Fielding and me. But it's a funny thing, Miss Rosamund, the minute after you'd rung up and told me it was you coming and not—not that other one—I had the feeling it wouldn't somehow happen. I just felt it, in my bones. I said to myself: there's something funny about it, I said. . . . But you know, Miss Rosamund, Mrs Fielding was a little bit put about when you never turned up, not you nor that other one. But I told her, I said I'd had a feeling all along it would end up like that."

Rosamund could have hugged the old woman. "That other one"—what wonderful, restrained, dignified disapproval the title conveyed! Rosamund realised how much she had feared that by now it would be "Miss Lindy!" Dear, faithful Jessie, how could she have suspected her of such treachery?

Mrs Fielding senior came out of the drawing room.

"Ah, there you are, Rosamund!" she exclaimed. "Isn't it turning cold? Come along in here, dear, and get yourself warm. Some coffee, Jessie, please, for both of us. Nice and hot."

"Yes, Madam. Thank you, Madam." Jessie melted into the kitchen; and soon Rosamund and her mother-in-law were settled one on each side of the bright log fire, sipping coffee, and talking about Mrs Fielding's book.

"She's been such a help to me, you know, dear, your friend Lindy. *Such* a pity she's gone away like this, without warning any of us, just when I was beginning to get my notes about the First Period in order. But of course you young people are so busy nowadays, always rushing about . . . and no doubt she'll be back very soon. It's the charts, you see; and then there's this second section all ready for typing any time now——Not in its *final* form, you understand, Rosamund, but it's *such* a help to see it clearly typed out, even if it's only rough notes."

"I'm sure it is. But, Mother, why didn't you ask *me* to do it? I can type, you know."

Rosamund tried to speak lightly, not to show how hurt she had been. Mrs Fielding looked surprised.

"Why, my dear, of course I'd have asked you, but you weren't *there,* were you? And then when your friend Lindy told me how busy you were, and how you wouldn't have any time for it till after Christmas. . . ."

"Did she say that? As a message from me?"

Mrs Fielding seemed a little impatient.

"Yes, yes; but it didn't matter, dear, not the least bit. I know what a lot you must have on your hands, all you young people have; and all I wanted was that *someone* should do it. She turned out to be most capable—and so kind. The only nuisance is, that she should have gone away just *now.*"

"But—I mean, she doesn't know much about it all, does she?" Rosamund blurted out, unable to keep the jealousy out of her voice. "She doesn't know Greek, or anything?"

"Well, dear, nor do you," replied Mrs Fielding equably. "But that hasn't stopped *you* being the greatest of help to me all these years, has it? She helped me in the same sort of way as you do—she seemed to have just the same knack. I suppose that's why you're such good friends —a similarity of outlook—the way your minds work. A splendid basis for friendship. . . ."

"I suppose so," replied Rosamund evenly, bending down and throwing a sliver of bark on the fire so as to hide her face. Here was yet another person finding likenesses between herself and Lindy! What nonsense—it was just that Lindy was cunning, was able, for her own purposes, to act a part. But then so was Rosamund—goodness, what else had she been doing over these past months? But that was different. To try and hide from your husband that you are jealous is in a different category from pretending to be kind and helpful to an old lady when really you are a scheming, two-faced . . .

Pretending? A dreadful uncertainty seized Rosamund. How did she know that Lindy was pretending? Suppose Lindy really was a kind and helpful person, but just a bit sharp-tongued? Her small kindnesses in the past had been legion, if one was simple-minded enough to take them that way; and as for her sharp tongue—that, too, was susceptible of more than one interpretation. Looking back, Rosamund could remember dozens of times when Lindy's remarks could have been taken either way—at their kindly face-value, or as subtle shafts and jibes. Always, Rosamund had interpreted them in the latter way; but could this have been just her own jealous imagination? *Could* it, possibly?

Again, waves of unreasoning anger swept Rosamund; as if Lindy had deliberately been a kind and helpful character in order to make it all the wickeder of Rosamund to have murdered her: and again Rosamund understood—though she could not feel—the absurdity of such anger. The absurdity of it all, really, because of course she hadn't murdered Lindy, and of course Lindy hadn't been either kind or nice, no indeed she hadn't: no need to rake the past for facts and proofs, to summon in review all those double-edged conversations. Instinct was enough. . . .

". . . So if you wouldn't mind, dear, since you *are* here, I'd like to go through just this last page. Geoffrey's old typewriter's still upstairs, you know, in the boxroom, if you wouldn't mind fetching it, then we could get down to it before lunch."

"Of course, Mother. I'd love to." Rosamund was wholly relieved at this interruption to her thoughts, which now seemed to be revolving fruitlessly in circles. She was also delighted at being pressed into service once more—why, it must have been for this that her mother-in-law had rung up so urgently last night! As she carried the heavy, old-fashioned typewriter downstairs she smiled at the old lady's impatient zest for her ambitious venture.

"I'm so glad you asked me to come," she said, as she eased the great clumsy thing onto the polished table. "I've been feeling awfully left out of all the excitements!"

"Asked you?" Mrs Fielding looked vague for a moment. "There's no need for you to wait to be *asked,* Rosamund, I'm sure you know that, dear; I'm always delighted to see you. I'm certainly very glad you've come, *particularly* glad this time, because it'll set Jessie's mind at rest; at least I hope so. She's been worrying about you the last few days, I'm sure I don't know why. She's got some idea that you're in some trouble or something—*I* don't know. I sometimes think Jessie is getting rather fanciful, but of course I don't like to upset her, telling her so. Anyway, she seems to be worrying about you, wondering if you are all right, all kinds of nonsense. There *isn't* anything wrong, is there, dear?" She glanced up sharply for a second, then began busying herself with her papers once more. "You would tell me, wouldn't you, if there was anything wrong? Not that I'd be much help, I'm too selfish, and I get more selfish as I get older, I know it very well. But I'd always be on your side."

From such an undemonstrative woman the words were extraordinarily moving, and Rosamund was filled with comfort.

"I know you would, Mother," she said gratefully. "But it's all right. There isn't any trouble . . . exactly. It's just that we're worried about Lindy disappearing. . . ."

"Oh, is *that* all!" Mrs. Fielding seemed greatly relieved. "Oh, well, that's all right, then, isn't it? She's sure to be back soon. *Such* a nice girl, and with a little home of her own to come back to, though it's a pity, in a way, that she's never married. Still, I'm sure she knows her own mind best, and marriage does mean a woman's giving up her freedom, even nowadays, there's no getting away from it. As you know, Rosamund, I loved Geoffrey's dear father very dearly, and no one could have been more deeply grieved than I was when he passed away, but all the same, I wouldn't go back to it, not for anything in the whole wide world. Well, anyway, dear, if you'd just have a look at this page—from *here* onwards. And then I've got a couple of paragraphs of the introduction I could get into shape while you're here. . . ."

Under the stimulus of Rosamund's presence and typewriting skill, the couple of paragraphs expanded into a number of forceful quarto pages. They worked steadily until one o'clock, when the soft peal of the gong summoned them ceremoniously to veal cutlets, mashed potatoes and sprouts, followed by treacle sponge. Like

many women of her generation, Mrs Fielding had re-
tained an immense gusto for nursery puddings of all
kinds; and in this particular setting Rosamund found that
she enjoyed them too.

After lunch they went back to the typing, and so ab-
sorbing did the task become that it seemed hardly any
time before the early winter dusk began to fall, and Jessie
came in with her gently clinking trolley, made up
the fire with fresh, sparkling logs, and drew the curtains
cosily against the encroaching night.

For a second Rosamund remembered that, for her, this
secure and cherished cosiness was but a temporary
thing. Soon—very soon—she would have to go forth into the
gathering damp and fog that was being so deftly obliterated by this soft, heavy swish of curtains. Then she
relaxed, resolved to enjoy to the full her last hour or two
in this enclosed paradise of safety and comfort.

After tea, as was her settled custom, she went out to
Jessie in the kitchen, and settled herself at the kitchen
table in readiness for the usual talk about Jessie's nieces.
Everything seemed exactly as usual, the Aga murmuring,
the kitchen warm and neat and shining, Jessie enjoying
her hour of leisure.

Yet there was something that was not the same. The
first inkling Rosamund had of this was when she found
that Jessie seemed, for the first time ever, to have nothing
to say about the Australian nieces. Rosamund tried one
lead after another, asking about this one and that one . . .
the one whose husband was on night work . . . the one
whose little boy was ever so smart, top of his class in
everything . . . the one who was to be X-rayed to see if
she was having twins: but even this met with no awakening of interest. What was the matter? Was Jessie ill?

"Are you ill, Miss Rosamund?" Jessie blurted out, suddenly and bewilderingly; then, evidently overcome by
the temerity of such a direct question, she began to apologise. ". . . If you'll excuse the liberty, but you aren't looking the thing at all, not at all. You look real poorly."

Why must Jessie say all this, all over again? Even
if it was true, did she have to harp on it? Rosamund's
irritation at the old servant's concern was out of all proportion . . . and quite suddenly she knew that it was not irritation at all, but fear. What, exactly, did Jessie mean by

all these befogging circumlocutions—"not the thing" and "poorly"? Did she really mean that Rosamund looked ill, or did she mean . . . did she sense . . . ?

"Oh, I'm all right, Jessie. . . . Is that a new picture of Queenie's wedding . . . ?" On pretence of wanting to examine the photograph in question Rosamund got up and studied herself surreptitiously in the mirror that stood on the same shelf as the photographs.

Did she look ill—pale—as one might after 'flu? Or was it something else that Jessie had noticed? A look in her eyes of guilt . . . of fear . . . ? The hunted look, the haunted look of newly committed murder? Did Jessie perhaps even know something of what had happened on that vanished Tuesday afternoon . . . the afternoon when it was alleged that Rosamund had arranged to come here, and then had failed to come . . . ? When instead she had lain in bed at home dreaming savage dreams . . . or had she, savage dreams and all, sallied out into the fog?

How much did Jessie know—or guess—or wonder? And how much of what she knew would she ever venture to put into the restrained, respectful language that was the only speech she knew?

Rosamund stared deep into the shadowed mirror, trying to see in her face what Jessie saw, to guess what Jessie guessed; and the longer she stared into her own eyes, the queerer they seemed, the more meaningless, like a word that one reads over and over too many times. Round, and blank, and empty of all human feeling, like a doll's eyes . . . and now, with such intensity of looking, they had fallen out of focus . . . the headache was coming back. Rosamund drew away from the mirror, rubbed her eyes.

"She's very pretty, isn't she?" she remarked of Queenie's photograph, without a single glance at it; and came back to her place.

She was aware of Jessie's eyes still fixed on her, with an expression of indefinable unease.

"I don't think you should be stopping too late, Miss Rosamund," advised Jessie uncomfortably. "It's . . . not a nice night. Not a nice night at all." She opened the kitchen curtain a crack, and peered out. "The fog's coming up again something cruel. . . ." She went on staring into the blanketing greyness for nearly a minute, and when she turned back, Rosamund fancied she saw in the old disciplined features a look she had never seen before; a look of fear.

"I think you should go *now*, Miss Rosamund" the old servant repeated, with veiled and respectful urgency. "I really think you should, indeed I do! Perhaps it's not my place to be saying it, but there's something I don't like about this fog tonight. . . ."

"Ah, Rosamund, *there* you are!" Mrs Fielding put her head round the door. "If you wouldn't mind, dear, there's a little bit I want to alter in that paragraph about the shields. Just a difference of emphasis, that's all, it won't take us a minute. You see, I don't want to give the impression that it's *only* the new dating I'm questioning. . . ."

It took them a number of minutes: two and a half hours, in fact, counting the brief interval for the poached egg and milky coffee that always constituted Mrs Fielding's supper. By the time they had finished, Rosamund saw to her dismay that it was nearly half past eight.

"I *must* go!" she exclaimed. "If I miss that nine o'clock train, there'll be nothing for ages. I'd love to stay a bit longer, but I really mustn't——"

"I'll phone for a taxi for you: don't fuss, dear," remonstrated Mrs Fielding with the confident unflappability of the one who doesn't actually have to make the journey; and it was only after four or five minutes of fruitless dialling that she allowed herself to admit that there were no taxis available this foggy night.

"You *would* have thought that they'd run a better service in a place this size!" she fumed righteously, in an attempt to blur her own share in delaying Rosamund's departure. "But never mind, dear, the evening trains are always late. I'm sure you'll manage if you walk briskly."

CHAPTER XXII

It was the walking briskly that caused Rosamund her first twinges of apprehension. At least, that was what she told

herself as she hurried along the deserted road, listening
to the beat of her own footsteps, the only sound unmuffled
by the fog. If only those beats could have been slow, and
steady, and confident, it would never have occurred to
her to imagine that anything could be wrong. It was this
quick, hurried tap-tapping, the patter-patter of her own
high heels that gave her this sense of being pursued.

It was all nonsense, of course; no one was pursuing
her. Twice she had stopped dead in the middle of the
empty road, but of course there had been no sound, nothing to be seen: only the fog, palely swirling, softly and
unobtrusively obliterating sight and sound, enclosing her
ever more deeply in its soft, sinister caress.

Why sinister, for goodness' sake? It was Jessie's odd,
uncharacteristic forebodings that were making her feel
like this, of course. Mother had been quite right; Jessie
was getting fanciful; though it was a pity, all the same,
that the conversation had been interrupted at just that
moment, before Jessie had had a chance to explain exactly what it was that was in her mind.

Rosamund hurried on, trying not to notice how relieved
she felt at the thought that she would soon be safely in
the High Street. There the lights would be shining, albeit
hazily, from the closed shop fronts. People would be
moving up and down, fumbling, laughing, suddenly friendly
as they encountered one another in this unfamiliar element.

But even the High Street seemed almost deserted by
now. The few footsteps that approached and passed seemed
as nervous, as hurried as her own. "Good evening!" the
anonymous voices called through the greyness, in search
of mutual reassurance; and presently the far-off whistle
of a train reminded Rosamund that she had nearly
reached the corner of Station Road.

But why was her heart beating like this, with the deep,
heavy throbs of sudden shock? Why did she feel this
overwhelming impulse to run, and run, and run . . .
faster, faster . . . away, away, as one runs in dreams?
Away from what? Was it from herself—from her own
guilt? Is it true that most fear is, basically, a fear of
oneself, of one's own impulses? This fear, the like of which
she had never felt before, was it a very ancient and familiar fear really—mankind's primitive fear of blood-guilt?

Was it the Furies of ancient Greece, the Avengers, who were pursuing her now through this foggy twentieth-century town? And was it for the murder of Lindy that they were pursuing her? Surely nothing but guilt, black and inescapable, could account for such sickening, overwhelming terror without material cause?

If she had indeed killed Lindy, she must expect to feel like this, perhaps for all her life long. As the years went by, there would be periods of forgetfulness, but they would never last for long. An hour?—two hours? Even a day? . . . and then on she would have to run again, on, on, through the nights and days, her guilty conscience pursuing her for ever.

Or could the pursuer be something even more strange, even more incomprehensible than conscience? Could it be Lindy's ghost itself hunting her along the foggy roads; invisible, implacable, sure, in the end, of victory, as Lindy had been sure in life? Was it Lindy's ghost that had hovered this evening outside the window of Jessie's kitchen, radiating unease out of the fog; and fear, and deadly premonition?

How easy it would be to begin to believe such nonsense, if one once let down the guards! Rosamund forced herself to move forward at a slow, even pace, for she knew now that this was the only way in which she could trust herself not to break into crazy flight. She listened to the steady steps, telling herself: Listen, it's all right, hear how steadily she's walking, a woman perfectly calm and unafraid. The beat beat beat of her feet feet feet, on and on and on, it can't go on for ever, soon she will be at the station, boarding the train for home. . . .

But when she got to the station, the nine o'clock train had gone. There was something almost consoling about the sleepy triumph with which the booking clerk informed her that there wouldn't be another train for an hour and a half, and that even then it would be a very slow one, not reaching London till after midnight. At least this was a form of human contact. Her idiotic, baseless panic began to subside. When the clerk had disappeared into the bit of booking office round the corner that the passenger can never see, she longed for him to come back, even if it were only to tell her that after all there wouldn't be a train till five in the morning, and that all the waiting rooms had to be locked up at ten sharp, it was the regulations, and she would have to sit out on the platform all night.

But he didn't; and she was able to creep into the empty, ill-lit waiting room and sit crouched over the burnt-out stove, as if to absorb from it memories of past warmth. But it wasn't the cold that she minded most, nor yet the slow, yellowish fingers of fog that drifted and coiled through the doorway, as though they, too, were seeking hopelessly for warmth. It was the smell.

Odd that it should affect her like this, for it was only the perfectly ordinary smell of railway stations—clammy—sooty—oily; not pleasant, admittedly, but surely not frightening either? Frightening in a strange way, too. The senseless panic of a few minutes ago was gone now that she was safely at the station, but it was replaced by a heavy, shapeless dread, of which this smell seemed to be the very heart and core. Fear and the smell together drifted round her, lazily intertwined, like smoke, filling her lungs, her senses . . . and then she began slowly to know that she had felt like this before.

When? Where? Waves of memory, like sickness, heaved against her consciousness, but she could not quite grasp them; and presently, as her nostrils grew accustomed to the smell, its power of evocation faded; the half-glimpsed memories submerged once more and were gone.

She must have fallen into a doze, for the next thing she knew, she was waking from a brief dream of confused and fearful tumult, to find that her train had just come to a standstill outside. In panic haste, heart still thumping from the shock of sudden waking, she snatched up her possessions, dashed out onto the platform and onto the waiting train.

But after all she need not have hurried. Nothing happened at all. It was the *slow* train, of course, as the booking-clerk had so gleefully predicted, and for what seemed a long, long time it stood there motionless. Once or twice a compartment door slammed somewhere further up: a porter called out "O.K., Mate!": then silence again.

Rosamund must be almost the only passenger on this train. It was an eerie feeling. After a while she got up from her seat and strolled along the corridor and back to see if there was anyone in any of the other compartments, but they were all empty—in her coach, at least, and it seemed really too silly to walk the whole length of the train just for the sake of seeing if anyone else was there. So she came back to her original seat, and sat there staring out through the mist at the empty, dimly-lit platform, waiting for something to happen. Probably the delay was something to do with the fog, but it was somehow unnerving, especially with everything so quiet. Why couldn't they at least throw bags in and out of the guard's van and shout at each other, the way they usually do on standing trains?

Her relief when she saw that there was, after all, another passenger, was absurd. He came panting along the platform, suitcase swinging, at something as near to a run as his short, elderly legs could manage; and it was all Rosamund could do not to call out a joyful welcome to him from her carriage window. Desperately he wrestled with the door two away from hers—evidently he was imagining, as she had once, that the train might be actually going to move—dragged it open, and bundled himself pell-mell inside.

Here he must have faced anti-climax as the train remained silent, immobile. He must have experienced, too, the same feeling of uneasy solitude as had oppressed Rosamund, for a minute later he appeared from along the corridor, peering rather sheepishly into her compartment before he came in and settled himself behind his newspaper in the furthest possible corner from her.

Rosamund felt immense fellow-feeling for her silent, well-barricaded companion. He had deliberately chosen the only compartment on the train with someone in it, and had then, equally deliberately, proceeded to fence himself off from all possible contact. Evidently he wanted exactly what she wanted—the solace of knowing that someone else existed, but not the bother of talking to them. Dear, nice, elderly gentleman! thought Rosamund, although all she could see of him was a pair of dark, well-creased trousers and black polished shoes.

As though it had been waiting politely all this time for him to settle down, the train now wheezed and groaned into movement, and as it slowly gathered speed, Rosamund felt a rush of even greater thankfulness for her silent companion.

For the fear had come upon her again. With the throbbing of the wheels it had come back . . . it grew, and throbbed, and mounted until she nearly screamed aloud. What it would have been like to be alone with it on this empty train was something she could not dare to imagine. She fastened her eyes on those prosperous neat legs, those reassuring shiny shoes, and waited for the spasm of terror to pass, as if it was a physical pain.

And pass it did. The train settled to an even pace, nosing its way leisurely through the fog, and Rosamund relaxed sufficiently to think of getting out her book. Not to read, exactly, she knew her mind was too preoccupied for that, but the mere sight of print on her lap would be reassuring. Also, it would set her companion's mind at rest should he venture to peer round his newspaper and look at her. It would be dreadful if he saw her looking unoccupied, and was frightened out of the compartment by the fear that she might say something.

Presently the train began slowing down again; it was wandering into yet another little country station; and now, to her horror, Rosamund saw that her dear elderly gentleman was folding his paper. Yes, he was picking up his hat . . . his gloves . . . he was reaching for his suitcase. . . . Ye gods, he was *going!*

She could hardly believe the horror of it. She could have fallen on her knees on the dusty, cigarette-strewn floor, begging him, praying him, to stay on the train. But no; all that her upbringing would permit her to do was to sit prim and reserved in her corner, smile politely when he murmured "Excuse me" as he pushed past her. And now he was opening the door . . . shutting it again behind him . . . fading, vanishing, with short, ungainly steps, into the fog.

Now she was alone. As the train lurched forward once more, she could feel the fear inside her mounting, gathering strength, rising from her stomach to her heart to her throbbing, shuddering mind. . . . And now the train was moving faster, crashing, thundering along the rails . . . it gave a great roaring whistle, like the howling of all the fiends in hell; and in that moment Rosamund remembered everything.

Yes, everything: right up to the stunning blow on the

head that had blacked out her memory of that Tuesday
afternoon.

CHAPTER XXIII

Tuesday. The Tuesday when she had been in bed with 'flu.
It was lunch time . . . no, early afternoon . . . and she
was roused from a feverish doze by the sound of the back
door opening.

"Rosie!" came the gay, unmistakable call. "Are you
there, Rosie?"

It was part of the irritating matiness between the two
households that they could walk in and out of each other's
houses unannounced. Rosamund clutched her dressing
gown about her and cowered, like a trapped animal, waiting to see what would happen. If she didn't answer,
would Lindy go away?

"Rose—ee!"

The voice sounded from the foot of the stairs, purposeful. In another moment steps would be coming up. Rather
than be caught here, in bed, Rosamund would go down
and face her.

"Oh—Hullo! Not up yet? Or are you not well, or something, you poor thing?"

Lindy was observing her from the foot of the stairs, and
her pitying tones seemed to Rosamund to embrace both
possibilities: that Rosamund was so slatternly as not
to get up till the afternoon, or that she was a middle-
aged, sickly sort of a creature, always succumbing to
various ailments.

"No, of course not! I've just been having a bath, that's
all," lied Rosamund, and felt her temperature leap in
protest. "I'm fine."

"Oh. Oh, well, I just came to say, could you tell Geoff
not to worry about his mother, I'm going down there this
afternoon. I know he was afraid she'd be disappointed
at my not going yesterday, she does count on it so, but I
just couldn't in all that fog."

"Counts on it so"! —just as if *she* was the daughter-in-law! Rosamund's anger broke through the lethargy of illness.

"Don't bother," she said icily. *"I'm* going this afternoon. I was just getting ready."

Nothing had been further from her thoughts until this moment, but as she spoke she knew that this was exactly what she would do.

"Oh." For one pleasing second Lindy looked quite disconcerted. Then a strange, almost a cunning look came into her eyes. "Oh, I see. How will you go, then?"

"By train, of course," snapped Rosamund. "Just as I have for about twenty years, before you turned up with your car."

Ordinarily she would never have allowed the hostility to sound in her voice like this, but her raised temperature, combined with anger, was making her feel not exactly light-headed, but a little irresponsible; a not unpleasant feeling, rather like being slightly drunk.

"Oh." Lindy had an oddly thoughtful look. "Well, that's that, then. I'd better go back."

Lindy had said goodbye. The back door had closed behind her, yet somehow Rosamund could not feel that she was really gone. She felt every minute that Lindy was going to walk in again, call some gay, sharp-edged comment up the stairs; so she prepared for her expedition with nervous, almost furtive, haste. Just as she was about to start, it occurred to her that she had better ring her mother-in-law and warn her that it was she, and not Lindy, who would be coming.

It was Jessie who answered the phone, and in a husky, nervous voice (nervous because of her fear that Lindy might somehow be overhearing her) Rosamund explained hastily the change of plan—stated it, rather, for explanation, really, there was none. Jessie understandably sounded a little bewildered, but never mind, Rosamund could think up some suitable explanation when she actually arrived there.

She didn't know then, of course, that she never would arrive.

Her memories of the next hour or so were a little blurred. She remembered that by the time she left the house the short December afternoon was already fading; and as she hurried along the damp, darkening streets, she presently became aware of footsteps hurrying just behind.

Yes, it was Lindy, swift and purposeful, full of some explanation or other of her presence . . . that she felt she ought herself to bring the typed notes to Mrs Fielding . . . that it was still too foggy for the car . . . that she thought it would be fun to travel down by train with Rosamund. . . .

As far as she could recall, Rosamund had managed to respond with reasonable civility . . . they had reached the station together . . . and there, yes, there had been Norah, just as she had claimed, chattering despairingly about Ned and his escapade. And then the train for Ashdene had come in . . . and the next thing Rosamund clearly recalled, she and Lindy were sitting opposite each other in an empty carriage, arguing. No, quarrelling, as they had never ventured to do before.

What had started it all? Had Rosamund, with the irresponsibility of fever, allowed her self-control to slip? Or had Lindy provoked it, with quiet deliberation, for purposes of her own? Whichever it was, Rosamund's next clear recollection was of bitter words darting back and forth between them, shrill above the clatter of the train.

"I *knew* you'd come to it in the end!" Lindy was crying triumphantly. "As soon as I saw you in that dressing-gown today, I knew you'd sunk to the last resort of the jealous wife—flight into illness. You were planning that Geoffrey should come home and pity you—feel guilty at having neglected you——"

The very thing which Rosamund had so absolutely determined *not* to do, from the very moment that she knew she was ill. Strange that Lindy should have put her finger on exactly that.

"What rubbish! I told you, I was getting ready to go out. And why on earth *should* I want Geoffrey to pity me? You don't really imagine I'm jealous, do you? Of *you*?"

She tried to put into the last word all the belittling scorn which Lindy would have done, but was conscious of failure. Lindy gave a pitying little laugh, inaudible above the roar of the train, but unmistakable.

"Jealous? Of course you're jealous—you're half crazy

with jealousy! It sticks out a mile, the way you've been acting tolerant all these months; encouraging Geoffrey to spend half his time with me; inviting me over to your place all the time; pretending I'm your best friend. Don't you know it's the oldest technique in the world? Practically all jealous wives do it—and they all think they're the only ones in the world ever to have thought of it! Just as you thought *you* were. . . ."

The truth in this was terrifying.

"Rubbish!" said Rosamund again, aware of how feeble it sounded. "I'm never jealous, ever. Ask Geoffrey——"

"Oh, *Geoffrey*! Poor Geoffrey! The man is always the last to see through a trick like that, I grant you! It makes me wild—it makes me absolutely *furious*—to have to stand by and watch him taking it all at its face-value, and thinking what a tolerant wife you are, and how he ought to be grateful to you, and not do anything to hurt you! But I'm not going to stand by and watch it any longer! I'm going to find a way of showing him what you're really like—jealous—spiteful—possessive! Just like the other wives! I'm going to talk to him this very night. . . . Tell him . . . !"

"And *I'm* going to tell him what *you're* really like!" cried Rosamund, fever and anger together blazing like fire in her body, giving her a sense of extraordinary abandon. "It makes *me* furious to watch him taking *you* at your face-value! I shall tell him that all this calm and gaiety that you lay on is just so much play-acting. I'll show him —prove to him that underneath you're nervy—hag-ridden —jealous. Yes, *you're* the jealous one! That's why you're always flattering the husbands and criticising the wives— it's because you know you can't make a man happy yourself, and so you're for ever trying to prove that nobody else can——"

The heat playing in her face was unbearable. With a quick movement Rosamund stood up, opened the window and leaned out, letting the blessed, cool, misty air stream across her face. Lindy's words about the obviousness of her jealously had struck too near the bone. In her fury, she only hoped that her own retaliatory words had struck Lindy with equally painful nearness.

They had.

At first, Rosamund was not aware of the hand reaching

softly, lightly, from behind as she leaned out . . . and by the time she knew that it was on the handle of the carriage door, turning it, it was too late. She tried to push Lindy violently away, but already the latch had slipped, and the only effect of her pushing was to speed her own falling outwards as the door swung open. It seemed like the ineffectual pushing of a dream, with no force, no impact . . . and then, strangely, she seemed to be floating away from the train, with no sense of violence, or even of rapid movement. During that half second, which was all it could have taken, she did not feel as if she was falling at all, but rather as if she was hovering, in utter freedom, while the lights and sparks of the train whirled past like wheeling stars. And it was not fear that she was conscious of at all, in that strange, disembodied instant; rather it was triumph; an exultant, glorious sense of victory. "I've won! I've won!" she seemed to cry aloud in her soul. "Now at last Geoffrey will know that she is wicked—evil! He will know that she is a murderer!' And as she glimpsed Lindy's white face, still leaning from the train as it streamed away from her, she felt that it was Lindy, not she, who was hurtling to her doom.

Less than a second, less than half a second, it must have been while she seemed to float thus like a triumphant, disembodied spirit; and then the ground, like some dark monster out of the fog, sprang up and flung itself upon her.

It must have been hours later when she recovered consciousness, and found herself lying among a tangle of bushes and tussocky grass by the railway line.

And now as Rosamund relived the memory, sitting once again in a train thundering through the misty night, the relief was so enormous that she could only close her eyes and lean back in a peace of mind and body that she had hardly expected ever to know again. Everything was explained now: her own blackout of memory; Lindy's disappearance; everything. After such a deed, Lindy could not do otherwise than disappear, at least for a time. And Rosamund must have had concussion from her fall, hence the temporary loss of memory, and also the savage headaches which she might have guessed, had she thought about it, were far worse than one would have expected from a mild attack of 'flu.

And those sickening panics that had so mysteriously assailed her of late—they were not, after all, a symptom of subconscious guilt—they were quite simply her nerves and body remembering the shattering shock of being flung from the train. For it was the sound of a train that had set them off on each occasion—the sound, or the sight, or the smell of trains and railways. Hence her inexplicable terror the other night when she had come with Basil to the railway bridge, and she had fancied that it must be something about his words or presence that was making her feel faint with fear.

The muddy shoes and coat were explained, too; and Lindy's battered handbag. Rosamund must have clutched at it in a last unnoticing effort to save herself; and Lindy, in the stress of the moment, or in fear of being pulled out herself, must have loosed her hold on it. Hence, perhaps, the frightened look on her face as it whirled away—even in that first second she must have realised that the handbag, found by Rosamund's body, would incriminate her beyond hope of escape.

Yes, what *would* Lindy have been thinking, in that moment and later? There could be no doubt that she had meant to kill Rosamund; but how soon did she realise that she had failed? It had been the merest chance that Rosamund had landed among grass and bushes—almost anywhere else, she would undoubtedly have been killed.

So what would Lindy have done, when she finally got off the train? Rosamund put herself in Lindy's place: she set her mind working as Lindy's mind must have worked, noticing, as she did so, how easily it came to her.

Well, of course, first and foremost she would try to get the whole thing regarded as an accident—you didn't need to have any particular sort of mind to decide on *that*. She couldn't pretend that she hadn't been on the train at all, because Norah had seen her; would it be best to pretend that she had witnessed the accident, or that she hadn't? Hadn't, of course; for if she had, then she should surely have pulled the communication cord at once. It would be easy enough to say that Rosamund had gone off down the corridor, and that it was some time before she, Lindy, began to wonder why she hadn't come back.

So what then? Well, of course, when she got out at Ashdene, she really *would* have to go through the motions of wondering why Rosamund hadn't got out too. She would have to show due concern about the disappearance.

Show who? There would be no point in all this pantomime of solicitude unless someone knew of it. Yet she certainly wouldn't want to alert the station people, have them sending search parties along the line before she had been able to retrieve the incriminating handbag. So at this point it would be a good idea to phone Geoffrey, let him know that something had happened, and that she, Lindy, was duly anxious about it; but not to tell him exactly *what* had happened yet, because she still wouldn't have a proper story worked out—later on she could explain the cryptic nature of her communication by claiming that she'd been so bewildered—couldn't think what had happened —didn't want to worry him without cause—that sort of thing.

A becoming degree of anxiety on her part thus established, she could now concentrate on retrieving the handbag. How long would this take? How far away from Ashdene had the "accident" occurred? And would Lindy go on foot—perhaps for miles? Or on a slow, infrequent country bus? Or would she dare to take a taxi to somewhere in the vicinity, with the risk of the taximan remembering about her if it came to being questioned by the police?

Whichever it was, it must have taken quite a long time; and by the time she got there Rosamund must have recovered consciousness and gone, still clutching the bag mechanically. . . . Rosamund could vaguely remember now, wandering, staggering over rough ground . . . darkness . . . confusion . . . lights . . . a telephone box. A blurred, dream-like attempt to phone Geoffrey, to summon his comfort and support. Rosamund felt strangely moved to know that it must have been from her, and from no one else, that he had received that sense of telepathic communion down the wires. And after that she must, somehow, have made the familiar journey home—so familiar after all these years that she could indeed have made it almost in her sleep.

So Lindy, after a long and anxious search along the railway bank, must have found that her victim, and the tell-tale bag, had both vanished. She would have known, then, that Rosamund must be still alive—or else that her body had already been found. Whichever it was, all hope of benefitting from her crime must in that moment have left her.

No, not *all* hope. Everything would depend now on how much Rosamund, if still alive, remembered about the accident. Lindy would no doubt realise that she might have been so shocked and stunned as not to remember anything at all—as indeed was the case, for a few days at least. Or Lindy might calculate that Rosamund would remember the fact of falling from the train, but might have been too confused to have noticed or remembered that Lindy had deliberately caused it. In which case, it could all still pass as an accident.

But Lindy must *know*. How would she set about finding out? She would keep telephoning the house anonymously until she heard Rosamund's voice answering . . . and then again she would telephone to find a time when no one was there so that she could slip in and retrieve her much-needed handbag. And all the time she would be trying to devise some way of finding out how much Rosamund remembered—how much she had divulged. Every day that there was nothing about it in the papers must have brought her a fraction more of reassurance. Sooner or later, as the risks of disclosure seemed to grow less, she might even venture to come back—watchful, cautious, armed with some clever and infinitely adaptable story to fit onto whatever turned out to be the known facts. Oh, she was clever enough; no doubt she would get away with it—especially with someone anxious to believe the best as Geoffrey would be.

And then everything would go on as before? Could it, with what Lindy knew . . . with what she must wonder, in the depths of the dark nights, whether Rosamund knew, too, even if nothing was ever said again? Always, on top of her hatred of Rosamund, there would now be fear added as well. You don't need actually to be a blackmailer to inspire this kind of fear . . . you only need to be in a position where you *could* be a blackmailer.

But of course, as things were, it was much simpler than this. Now that Rosamund really did remember the whole thing, she would go straight home and tell Geoffrey,

and they could then decide together what to do—if anything. That seemed hardly to matter. The real death-blow
to Lindy's hopes was that Geoffrey should know. All she
could do now was to stay invisible—go abroad—something
like that. Perhaps she had already done so. . . .

Some sound, some uneasy sense of movement, made
Rosamund open her eyes. Someone was standing out there
in the corridor . . . a face was pressed against the window
of the compartment. Lindy's face.

CHAPTER XXIV

For as much as half a minute after their eyes had met,
Lindy still did not move. She's trying to guess from my
expression how much I know, how much I remember,
Rosamund thought calmly, and without any sense of
danger. The immensity of her relief at discovering that
she was not the guilty one was still flooding her spirit,
leaving no room for any other emotion. She even smiled
at the white, watching face, in foolish gratitude that it,
and not her own, must for ever carry the marks of murder.

Slowly, Lindy slid open the compartment door and came
inside, closed it carefully and deliberately behind her;
and now Rosamund saw that her face, far from carrying
marks of guilt, had a look of wary triumph. It was not
so pale, either, as it had looked at first, pressed so intently
against the glass; it was the hard, yellow electric light and
the shreds of yellow fog that had found their way in out
of the night, that created an illusion of pallor. Rosamund's own face must be looking the same. . . .

"So we meet again!" Lindy spoke carefully, never taking
her eyes off Rosamund's face as she sat down opposite
her. "How are you now?"

After being pushed out of the train? After my attack of
'flu? Lindy must be deliberately keeping it ambiguous,
probing to find out how much Rosamund remembered.
And I won't tell her! resolved Rosamund—not because

it had yet dawned on her that there was any danger in her situation, but simply from a childish satisfaction at finding herself for once in a position to make Lindy feel uncomfortable, instead of the other way round.

"I'm very well, thank you," she replied distantly. "And how about you? Where've you been all this time?"

Lindy ignored the question.

"You don't *look* well," she insisted. "And Jessie doesn't think you look well, either. You really should begin to take more care of yourself, Rosie, at your age. . . ."

The nerve of it! All Rosamund's resolution to keep Lindy in the dark were swamped by the familiar sense of baffled outrage.

"Well, I like that! After *you* . . . !"

She stopped; but it was too late. The end of the sentence, unspoken, rang plain enough between them. Rosamund realised that she had given herself away completely. Lindy knew, now, that she knew; that she remembered. But what was all this about Jessie? Had Lindy been eavesdropping out there in the fog, outside the kitchen window? Of course she had—and outside the drawing room window, too; she would have been a fool not to have seized—indeed to have sought out—such an opportunity. She would have learned, from the mere fact of its non-inclusion in the conversation, that Mrs Fielding and Jessie had not heard of anything so dramatic as Rosamund's having fallen out of a train, accidentally or otherwise. Would Lindy have deduced from this that Geoffrey hadn't heard of it either? Well, let her wonder!

"You're a funny, secretive creature, Rosie," said Lindy, with an air of compassionate wonder. "Anyone else who'd had an accident like that would have rushed home and told everyone all about it. *Certainly* they'd have told their own husband! Geoffrey's going to think it very odd, isn't he, when he hears about it first from *me*, after all this time! Or perhaps he's used to it? Perhaps you're always like that? To me, it seems a very queer sort of relationship, for a husband and wife. . . ."

"Of course I'd have told Geoffrey at once—if I'd remembered it!" cried Rosamund. "But when I first recovered consciousness I'd completely forgotten—it's like that, after you've been stunned. It takes several days before you remember. . . ."

And only now, as she watched the triumph glittering yellow in Lindy's face under the bare electric bulb, did she realise how completely she had fallen into the trap, and how incautious were these revelations that Lindy had surprised out of her by playing on her childish pride.

For Lindy had now been told, almost in so many words, not only that Rosamund had so far not incriminated her at all, but that she was proposing to do so as soon as they reached their journey's end. Now at last Rosamund saw quite clearly how very important it was to Lindy that she, Rosamund, should never reach that end of the journey. Once already Lindy had attempted her murder; the second time, perhaps, was even easier. . . .

Yet what could Lindy do? Certainly Rosamund wasn't going to lean a second time out of the window into the fog and the darkness. There was no way, now, in which Lindy could take her by surprise. All she had to do was sit here firmly, on her seat . . . not to be trapped into going near the window, or even into standing up at all . . . and then nothing could happen. After all, the journey couldn't go on for ever. In half an hour or so they would be in London. Just sit here then, immoveable, and let Lindy do her worst.

But Lindy just sat there, too. She had stopped speaking, and there was a tiny smile about her mouth. Rosamund watched it, uneasily, as if it was a small, bright weapon. What was Lindy thinking, planning?

"You think I'm planning to kill you, don't you?" said Lindy suddenly, and with curious scorn in her voice. "But I'm not, you know. I don't plan things. I act on impulse, always. You made me so furious. . . ."

Was it true? Rosamund remembered several little incidents, from the days and hours before that fatal afternoon, that suggested to her, now, that Lindy might have been planning it all, or at least have been waiting and watching for just such an opportunity. Her odd, half-guilty cross-questioning of Rosamund at Norah's coffee party: the carefully-chosen jibes which (perhaps predictably) stung Rosamund into travelling impetuously down to Ashdene in the fog . . . and with a temperature, too, which perhaps would make the "accident" seem less extraordinary, more explicable, than it would otherwise have been.

Not that it mattered now. Why was Lindy trying so emphatically to refute the imputation of forethought in all this, when it could make no possible difference one way or the other? Whether the attempted murder had been planned or unplanned was now of no importance or relevance.

Except to Lindy's pride. Even now, under the shadow of total disclosure, it was more important to Lindy to maintain her image of herself as a passionate, impulsive sort of person than it was to think of a way of getting herself out of the present impasse.

It would be to me, too, flashed through Rosamund's mind; and this small stab of fellow-feeling put her a tiny bit off her guard.

Off her guard against what? For Lindy was still sitting there, making no move, and the minutes were passing. Yet still the smile flickered round her mouth; she wore a look of curiously inappropriate confidence. Was this, too, merely part of an act?

"Besides," said Lindy suddenly, as if there had been no pause since her last words. "There are some things you will mind more than being killed——"

In a single swift movement (impulsive to the last?) she stood up and flung open the carriage door, and the foggy darkness, like a hurricane, poured in.

Was it a trap—an unwontedly clumsy trap? Was she expecting Rosamund to leap to her feet and try to close the door? Rosamund, as she had resolved, clung to her seat. Here, sitting down, she was surely safe . . . and then, as she sat there, she realised that Lindy was pulling the communication cord.

"It'll be your word against mine!" cried Lindy, her whole face aglitter with triumph; and then, quite calmly, she stood there waiting for the train to slow down.

Only then did Rosamund understand the import of it all. As soon as the train was going slowly enough for her to do it safely, Lindy was going to jump out, be found lying by the side of the line, saying that Rosamund had pushed her—and *then* what a feeble, implausible, cooked-up imitation would Rosamund's story of last Tuesday sound—coming, as it now would, *after* Lindy's?

Or was all this what Rosamund was meant to suppose . . . was it really just another trap . . . a cunning way to get

her to leave her seat and come to the doorway? No . . .
her first guess had been right . . . Lindy was indeed
preparing to spring as the train slowed down . . . slower
. . . slower. . . .

And then suddenly the expression on Lindy's face was
like nothing Rosamund had ever seen before. The train
was slowing down indeed, just as she had planned, but only
because it was coming into a station.

As a *femme fatale* Lindy had been very nearly convincing. As a murderess she had been superb; but she
had no ready-made image of herself appropriate to this.
As the guard, bored and irritable, came to ask her why
she had pulled the cord, she looked once more exactly as
Rosamund had first seen her, peering into the back of that
furniture van: a rather fussy, dumpy little woman.

The glittering façade was shattered; and Rosamund,
as she watched its disintegration, felt herself, too, to be
diminished: with the grief of a fellow-craftsman, she witnessed the smashing of so mighty a work of art.

After Lindy had gone abroad, which she did almost
at once, there seemed no point in making the affair public
—Geoffrey and Rosamund were entirely agreed on this,
from the very first. There was no point even in letting
Eileen know the whole truth—they both felt that Eileen had
enough on her mind already, in piecing together her marriage once again. One couldn't even expect her, in her still
delicate domestic situation, to take over Shang Low. So
for a while, before the new people came, Rosamund still
had to go in and out to feed him; until, gradually, it began
to seem easier to bring him into her house rather than take
the food into his; and even after that, it was still a good
many weeks before she fully realised that they now owned
a Pekinese. As the months went by, Shang Low came to
adore Geoffrey more and more, but he still continued to
display a measure of guarded contempt towards Rosamund.

But it didn't matter; for Geoffrey and Rosamund soon
decided that the best kind of Pekinese *always* adore their
masters and despise their mistresses. It became one of their
things.